I was missing Joe already and wondering (worrying) how I would survive without seeing him for six whole weeks. Would he forget me? I mean, we've only been a proper couple for a few weeks. And they do say that out of sight is out of mind. On the other hand they also say that absence makes the heart grow fonder. "They" should really get their stories straight.

TOTALLY FABULOUS

Michelle Radford

HARPER TEEN
An Imprint of HarperCollins*Publishers*

HarperTeen is an imprint of HarperCollins Publishers.

Totally Fabulous

For information address HarperCollins Children's Books, a division of HarperCollins Publishers, 10 East 53rd Street, New York, NY 10022.
www.harperteen.com

Library of Congress Cataloging-in-Publication Data
Radford, Michelle.
Totally fabulous / Michelle Radford. — 1st ed.
p. cm.
Summary: While attending a secret boot camp in New Jersey to hone her extrasensory skills, fourteen-year-old Fiona cannot resist using her new powers to "fix" the American relatives she has just met.
ISBN 978-0-06-128531-8
[1. Extrasensory perception—Fiction. 2. Family life—New Jersey—Fiction. 3. Eccentrics and eccentricities—Fiction. 4. Schools—Fiction. 5. Interpersonal relations—Fiction. 6. New Jersey—Fiction.] I. Title.
PZ7.R1174Tot 2009 2008035606
[Fic]—dc22 CIP
AC

Typography by Ray Shappell
09 10 11 12 13 LP/RRDH 10 9 8 7 6 5 4 3 2 1

First Edition

In memory of Jean Cunnah,
intrepid explorer, adventurer, and the bestest,
kindest mother-in-law a person could have.

Acknowledgments

A huge thank-you to Farrin Jacobs and Kari Sutherland for all of their wise and totally fabulous help with this book.

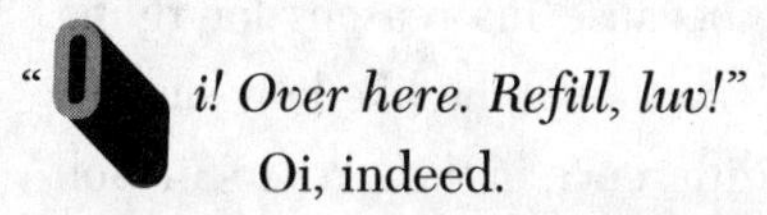

"*Oi! Over here. Refill, luv!*"

Oi, indeed.

When we were first planning this trip, William Brown *totally* should have listened to me when I suggested that we fly coach instead of first class to New York, because first class is too elitist and money wasting. And irritating-minor-celebrity attracting. A very minor, very, very irritating celebrity who goes by the name of Dude Mann. Who would willingly go by that name? I mean, where's the imagination behind that choice?

If only I could use my ESP power of compulsion to shut him up, but I can't, because (a) I can't control my powers properly yet, and (b) I promised William Brown (my long-lost now recently found father) I wouldn't try to use them until I've learned to control them—he's worried that I might harm someone (including myself).

"Did you see that episowde of *The Flat* where I challenged Jayda to a chocolate-eating contest, and she stuffed ten Snickers down that fat gullet of hers? Ha ha ha ha." Dude Mann, who is sitting two rows in front of us, is talking at the poor cabin assistant in his loud Cockney accent as she serves him yet another glass of champagne. *Talking at,* rather than *holding a conversation with,* because he's enthralled by the sound of his own voice. Unfortunately, he thinks that everybody else is, too.

"I'm kind of glad I missed that one," William Brown whispers across to me. "You know, I'm really beginning to wish I'd taken your advice that we fly coach instead." He rolls his eyes in the direction of Dude.

"Oh, no," I whisper back, because his reasons for flying first class were really great. Even though he liked my suggestion that he could donate the difference in the fares to Sir Bob Geldof's charity makepovertyhistory.com. "You fly so much between England and America that you're right, you need the comfort and space that first class offers, so that you arrive at your destination refreshed and ready to face whatever challenges may present themselves." That sounds so formal. I'm not entirely comfortable around William Brown yet, even though I like him a lot.

"There's no chance we'll arrive un-travel-weary and uncrumpled if we have to listen to Dude Mann for the entire trip," he tells me and laughs.

How nice was it, though, of William Brown to write a check for makepovertyhistory.com, anyway, to please me? William Brown donates to a lot of other charities, too, which is another reason why I like him very much. I mean, it would have been a huge disappointment if my dad had turned out to be a miserly philanderer or something.

I can't bring myself to call him Dad, yet. He told me to call him Will, but that seems strange, too. I've thought of him as William Brown for so many years, it's a hard habit to break.

Anyway, I just *knew* when I saw Dude Mann at first-class check-in earlier that he was going to ruin my first ever journey to America, because I got tiny warning prickles at the back of my neck. He was a *complete* nuisance on the celebrity version of the reality show *The Flat,* where ten complete strangers have to live together for months, without contact with the outside world. On his first day with the show he ate half the Flatmates' food rations, and disgusted everyone with his unhygienic personal habits, which involved him inserting fingers in certain facial orifices. Yuck! Would you do that on national TV?

I wish I'd warned William Brown that Dude could be a possible nuisance on the flight, but I couldn't because William Brown had to take an urgent business call on his mobile, and had therefore walked outside the main airport doors for some privacy. It was pretty noisy in Heathrow Airport, I can tell you, because July is the height of the holiday season. It was filled with people bustling here and there, not to mention the long queues.

Mum and her boyfriend, Mark Collingridge (who had come to wave me off), didn't even *notice* Dude Mann, because Mum was too busy hugging me and telling me how much she'd miss me (I will miss her, too), on account of me never having spent six weeks away from her before, and had I packed my cute T-shirt with the diamanté cat face on it? (Yes.)

Mark Collingridge also kept hugging me and telling me how much *he'd* miss me, too (which was sweet because he hasn't known me very long), especially our discussions about movies and books. Then he told me about a documentary he'd seen recently on passenger plane disasters. Honestly, I really like Mark Collingridge, but he does have a habit of recounting movies or books that somehow relate to my life—and never in a good way.

Like the time a few weeks ago when he insisted on discussing a book I was supposed to read for English, *Flowers for Algernon*, in which the main character takes part in a brain-enhancing experiment and becomes supersmart for a little while, then, tragically, begins to deteriorate. It was just after I discovered William Brown on the Internet, and my ESP powers had kicked in big-time (according to William Brown, a severe emotional shock like finding your long-lost father can cause a person's powers to develop suddenly). I hadn't plucked up the courage to confess my true identity to William Brown, and I was worried that my ESP powers were really a brain tumor because of the side effects (terrible pounding headaches and nausea, and sometimes I have to be sick).

While Mum and Mark Collingridge were talking to me and hugging me, Dude Mann was insisting to the airline assistant that excess baggage rules shouldn't apply to him—he was a celebrity after all and needed his full wardrobe available for his American TV debut. (That was a shock. Why was he even going to *be* on American TV?)

It was right about then that the warning prickles at the back of my neck got a bit stronger. I get these prickles when something is going to happen. Like the time Mr. Fenton, my math teacher, went on the school skiing trip and I got a bad feeling he would break a leg, and he did. Or the time when I found William Brown's website and I got a prickly feeling that he was my dad. Both of those times I got a precognitive moment coupled with the tingles, so I knew which one was bad (poor Mr. Fenton) and which one could be good (finding my dad). Dude isn't good news, so the prickles were probably bad on this occasion. *Was this my budding precognition warning me that our plane was going to crash? Or did the prickles mean that I was about to accidentally use my power of compulsion to stop Dude Mann from being such a pain and wish him to the moon or something?* That would not be a good thing. I was trying really hard to calm myself down and not borrow trouble.

That was difficult, because although I was really excited about the trip, I was feeling pretty emotional about plenty of other things, too. Things like, did Mum and William Brown still have feelings for each other, and had I done the right thing by contacting him? I mean, what if I accidentally caused two love triangles? Poor Mark Collingridge and poor Jessica Waterstone, William Brown's fiancée. Two lives potentially ruined!

Another thing I was worried about was would my new American family members like me? William Brown's been a bit evasive about them. He told me they could be a bit quirky and take some time to get used to, but he assured me that they'd love me once they got to know me. One thing Mum told me ages ago before I found William Brown that she remembered from their brief time together was that he'd had problems with his parents. Pretty much like Mum had problems with her mother, Grandmother Elizabeth (who can be very annoying and bossily baronessy, and Mum had even completely stopped talking to her until three years ago).

I was also missing Joe already and wondering (worrying) how I would survive without seeing him for six whole weeks. Would he forget me? I mean, we've only been a proper couple for a few weeks. And they do say that out of sight is out of mind. On the other hand they also say that absence makes the heart grow fonder. "They" should really get their stories straight. But as Joe said last night when we were saying goodbye, even though I will be in a time zone five hours behind England, there's always the Internet. He promised to e-mail and instant message as often as he can. I *so* wanted to tell him about ESP boot camp, and how for part of my American trip I wouldn't be around much during the day, which would mean that it would be late at night for him by the time I could e-mail or instant message back. I nearly blurted out the whole ESP thing. I improvised and told him I was attending science camp, which is not a lie but is not the whole truth—it *is* scientific. Joe totally approved of that. Then Joe kissed me and I forgot about everything except how lovely he is (and how weak at the knees his kisses make me feel).

I won't get to kiss him again for six whole weeks!

But here's the thing. How do you talk to a boy now that he is your boyfriend and not just your friend? I know that Joe really likes me, and we have a great time discussing stuff like the discovery of 700 new species of marine creatures in the hostile waters around Antarctica, and how it's amazing they can live in what was thought to be a barren abyss, but it's hard to tell (except for the kissing part) exactly how he feels. I mean, shouldn't we be saying mushy stuff to each other by now?

With all of that on my mind, Dude Mann was the last thing I needed to tip me over the ESP edge. Then the assistant patiently explained to Dude that normally it wouldn't be a problem for a first-class traveler, but twice the allowed weight was a bit over the top.

Twice the allowed weight would be more than 160 pounds of baggage! Who owns that many clothes?

I could feel myself getting really angry with him and upset for the assistant. First, he tried bribing her. Then he whined a lot about the unfairness of it all, and how she wasn't showing enough respect for him, and I wondered if he'd *ever* get checked in. The anger and prickles at the back of my neck intensified, and I could feel the now-familiar pressure building in my brain. This was bad. I really needed to calm down before I did something stupid.

Then, just as Mum was telling me not to worry about Daphne Kat, and promising not to feed her anything unhealthy-to-cats like General Tso's Chicken, and Mark Collingridge was advising me about what I should do in the event of a flight emergency, Dude Mann burst into fake tears and began to plead with the airline assistant.

I was nearly wishing that Dude really *would* fly to the moon and at the same time trying frantically to stop the power from building in my brain.

Then he threw himself on the floor in (fake) misery and told the assistant he wasn't going anywhere until she'd checked in *all* of his baggage, and how he was going to complain to her manager, the airport authorities, and the airline CEO himself.

Then he added that Richard Branson, billionaire president of Virgin Atlantic, was a personal friend.

Just as I thought I was going to burst with the effort of trying NOT to let the pressure build up even more in my brain, Mum stopped hugging me for long enough to take an envelope and a small packet wrapped in gold paper out of her bag and said, "Last night, Joe asked me to give this to you before you checked in."

The prickles dissipated instantly and I forgot all about Dude Mann, because I was totally suffused with my love for Joe! I wondered why he hadn't given it to me himself when he saw me last night. I assumed he wanted to avoid any mushy scenes.

I wanted to save the note and gift to open when I was alone, but Mum was all, "Go on, open it, Fiona, or I'll die from the suspense. The look on his face when he gave them to me was priceless." And Mark Collingridge was all, "Ah, young love." He smiled at Mum in such a soft, gentle way and touched the side of her face. Mum practically melted into a puddle right there in the airport! This kind of alleviated my fears about the two love triangles. And if Mark Collingridge and Mum could show emotion in a busy international airport, so could I.

I opened the note first. My heart nearly burst out of my chest when I read it. It said, "MarieCurieGirl, this is a small token to mark our first date. It also represents how long your trip will seem to me, how much I'll miss you, and how I will feel while you are gone. OccamsRazor."

MarieCurieGirl and OccamsRazor are our e-mail names and also our pet names for each other. I'm MarieCurieGirl because I really admire Marie Curie (who won two Nobel

Prizes, each in a different field of science). Joe's OccamsRazor suits him, too, because just like Occam's Razor in science, Joe has the habit of razoring off the bits you don't need in a given situation so that you have the simplest, most elegant explanation of the facts.

When I opened the packet I nearly cried. Inside was a necklace with a silver trilobite charm, so delicately crafted, complete with tiny legs and antennae. I understood Joe's cryptic note instantly. You see, our first date (although we didn't call it a date at the time) was to the Natural History Museum. But that's not what made me nearly dissolve into tears. Trilobites became extinct *250 million years ago*, and what Joe was telling me was that my trip would seem that long to him. He was also telling me that he would feel extinct, as in no longer alive, snuffed out like a candle, without me!

How romantic was that?

Mum and Mark Collingridge didn't ask to read the note, which was a relief, because some stuff is just private. Instead, Mark Collingridge insisted on fastening the trilobite chain around my neck right there and then, and as I lifted my hair out of the way, the prickles came back. . . .

Dude Mann, who was still throwing a tantrum at check-in, did a sudden about-face. He stopped midrant, got up from the floor, took his three huge suitcases from the weighing machine, put them back on the airport trolley, and wheeled them toward the airline help desk so that he could pay his excess baggage charge.

I could tell that the other passengers at the first-class check-in were surprised, because they were all watching him with expressions of amazement. Obviously, the check-in assistant couldn't believe it, either, because she was sitting there with her mouth wide-open.

It was then that I caught sight of William Brown in the corner of my eye. He was standing by the newspaper shop. He was also totally focused on Dude Mann, and a thought occurred to me.

Did William Brown use his powers of ESP on Dude Mann to make that happen? After everything he told *me* about not using ESP, except in exceptional circumstances?

Then, William Brown saw me watching him.

He winked at me and smiled!

I couldn't ask him about it, because we're not supposed to talk about ESP in public places in case we're overheard. I mean, I'm not even allowed to tell *Mum* about it.

After we'd said good-bye to Mum (who looked like she was going to cry, but didn't—she squeezed me fiercely instead and told me that I'd better get on the phone regularly or she'd be over the Atlantic in a New York minute to check on me and/or rescue me if needed) and gone through security, William Brown was all nonchalant and casual, saying things like, "Do you want a book or some magazines for the journey?" and, "I can't wait to show you America, you're going to love New York." Although he didn't say, "I just know you're going to love your new grandma, grandpa, aunt, and cousin," which was a bit unsettling.

Dude Mann also acted like nothing had happened. He just went back to his usual (irritating) self.

"Uh-oh, I don't think *that's* a good idea," William Brown tells me as Dude moves to the first-class bar area to entertain us all with more of his antics. When I say "entertain" I don't mean it in a good kind of way.

"Then she went this green spewey color, so green she was the color of vomited cabbage," Dude says to the posh woman in the sharp suit, who's just gone over and introduced herself to him. What was she *thinking*? Does she *like* trouble?

I didn't watch that particular episode (I can't bring myself to watch as much since Dude joined the show), but my stomach rolls as I picture this in my mind. I wonder if the sushi I had for lunch will be making a bid for freedom from my stomach sometime soon. I think *I* may be the color of vomited cabbage, too.

"Hey, are you feeling okay, Fiona?" William Brown asks me in his warm baritone American voice. "Do you need me to get you something? Some mineral water to settle your stomach?"

"How about a parachute?" I joke and try to muster up a smile.

William Brown laughs. "I think my ears may explode if I have to listen to too much more of this. Do you think America's ready for him?"

"I don't think England was ready for him, never mind America."

Then William Brown smiles encouragingly at me, and I think how ungrateful I am to be thinking horrible thoughts about minor celebrities, and how lucky I am to have found my father in the first place. Against needle-in-a-haystack odds!

It's a good job that I have my own portfolio and check the Internet daily for companies to invest in, because otherwise I'd *never* have stumbled on William Brown's company, Funktech, and therefore never would have stumbled across My True Father!

"The best part was when she puked all over the living room floor. Ha ha ha ha—did you ever see anyfing so funny and hilarious in your en-ti-yer life? Ha ha ha ha." Dude Mann laughs into Suit Lady's face, and a bit of spit flies out of his mouth. Suit Lady doesn't even seem to notice!

"Yuck. Is it me? How gross is that?" I ask William Brown.

"No, it's not you. Very gross. Tell me, because I missed this part. Is his name *really* Dude Mann?" William Brown grins at me, and his brown eyes crinkle kindly.

"Oh, yes—didn't you catch the millionth time he told us that he'd changed his name by deed poll to make it official?"

William Brown reaches across and squeezes my hand, and I get a little prickle at the back of my neck. It happens every time William Brown touches me; it's all to do with both of us having ESP, apparently.

"I think your idea of a parachute might be a good one." William Brown reaches into the bag of freebie goodies we got due to our first-class status. "But we're still two thousand miles from land, and I don't know about you, but I'm not up to swimming that far in freezing water. How about an alternate plan?" He holds out a pair of earplugs. "With some luck the champagne will soon knock him out, what do you think?"

I think that sounds good. I also think this might be a good way of discreetly inquiring about what happened earlier.

"Definitely." I look into William Brown's eyes so I don't miss any slight reaction. "Um, failing the champagne and earplugs, there are, you know"—I pause meaningfully—"other ways, too." Then I wrinkle my nose a bit, so that he'll understand my meaning (like Samantha in *Bewitched* when she performs magic. Except ESP's not as easy as wrinkling one's nose. If only!).

But William Brown just grins in an inscrutable, sphinxlike way. And winks at me again!

So did he or didn't he?

What else is a girl to do when she's confused, except discuss it with her best friend?

I might currently be cruising several thousand feet above the Atlantic Ocean, but one of the benefits of first class is that I have Internet access. And I can see that Gina's online.

I'm not supposed to discuss ESP at all in any kind of communications medium, even with other people who have ESP, because William Brown says that government agencies listen in on phone calls and spy on instant messages and e-mail, and what do you think they would do with people with ESP if they could get their hands on them? I totally agree, because I worry, specifically, what would they do with *me*?

I could be whisked off to a life of imprisonment and scientific experiment, and be forced to do things that I don't want to do, and my life would be OVER.

Or a crime gang might kidnap me and threaten to hurt someone I love if I don't perform nefarious deeds for them, like robbing a bank, or stealing government secrets to aid their cause, or something even *worse*, and my life would truly be OVER.

William Brown's Funktech computer network and phone system are secure, though, because otherwise how would he ever be able to communicate with other espees (people with ESP powers)? Of course, some of them can read minds so they don't actually *need* a physical communications system. How cool would it be to be able to communicate telepathically? That would actually be useful and *usable.*

Anyway, even though I didn't really tell Gina I have ESP, she's so empathic and in tune with me that she guessed. So, because of this vital communications embargo, Gina and I have come up with a cunning system of thwarting any authorities who might be spying on us. It's a game we call Corrupt a Wish. If I have any ESP moments, I tell Gina I made a wish and Gina will understand that it was one of my ESP moments.

MarieCurieGirl to Feminista: Hi, Gina.

Feminista to MarieCurieGirl: That was super quick! U've only been gone a few hours! R U in NJ already?

MarieCurieGirl to Feminista: No—the plane has Internet access.

Feminista to MarieCurieGirl: Wow! Buzzing! What's it like 2 B in 1st class? U lucky thing! Lots of room to self? Own entertainment system?? Must be minty!

Gina is very fond of teen slang. Mainly because the love of her life, Kieran, is also a slang guru. *Minty* and *buzzing* are just her ways of saying "cool."

MarieCurieGirl to Feminista: It's lovely. Like a posh hotel. The only non-minty thing is that Dude Mann's on the flight. Remember him?

Feminista to MarieCurieGirl: U R KIDDING ME! THE Dude Mann? Can U get his autograph 4 me?

MarieCurieGirl to Feminista: But you can't stand

him! You said he should be evicted after that episode of *The Flat* where Keith won laundry rights and Dude was so angry it wasn't him, he threw Keith's laundry out the window.

Feminista to MarieCurieGirl: I know, but he's compulsive viewing & how often do U get 2 C a famous person in real life, even if they R howlin?

MarieCurieGirl to Feminista: Oh, no! Now he's SEAT DANCING all over a guy in the bar area.

Feminista to MarieCurieGirl: ?? Like in the episode when he won the right to have his MP3 player for the day, & when everyone had gone to bed, he went around *The Flat* and woke up all the Flatmates by jumping on their beds and seat dancing all over them? Has he driven U to making any wishes, yet?

MarieCurieGirl to Feminista: Yes, I nearly wished he'd stop making a fuss at check-in earlier and go pay for his excess baggage like other people.

Feminista to MarieCurieGirl: Granted! U now have a terrible headache and need to take 2 Tylenol. Next wish?

MarieCurieGirl to Feminista: William Brown has a headache and I wish for 2 Tylenol for him, instead.

Feminista to MarieCurieGirl: WHAT? WB needs the Tylenol? Not U? Do U mean what I think U mean?

MarieCurieGirl to Feminista: Not sure. It's hard to tell because WB is Sphinx Reincarnate. Am keeping an open mind.

OccamsRazor to MarieCurieGirl: Hey, I can see you online. You there, MCG? Is it Really You?

Oh, it's Joe! My heart beats a bit quicker as I finger my silver trilobite. I love the way he remembers all our conversations. Once, before we were, you know, a couple, he came to talk to me by the lockers in school, and I was a total dork because I was so surprised, and said, "Oh, it's you." Since then he's kind of teased me about it and says things like it's Still Me (meaning him), or it's Really You (meaning me). Then I remember his lovely message and my trilobite necklace and feel a bit embarrassed. What do I say to him? This boyfriend/girlfriend stuff is *so* confusing.

MarieCurieGirl to OccamsRazor: Hi, OR! ☺. Yes, it's Really Me! Thank you for my trilobite necklace, it's lovely. Much better than any old Masiakasaurus knopfleri necklace.
OccamsRazor: ☺. You're welcome. It was a tough choice, but then I thought the Masiakasaurus alternative was too obvious. And only seventy million years ago . . .

This is one of the reasons why I know Joe and I are soul mates, even though Joe's not good at vocalizing his feelings. Who else would know about this dinosaur in the first place and understand my hidden meaning? See, it was named after Mark Knopfler from Dire Straits, and Joe would instantly get my connection to the music industry via Mum.

Feminista to MarieCurieGirl: BRB. Kieran's online . . . love calls!
MarieCurieGirl to Feminista: OK. Love's calling

my end, too. Joe's online! BTW, he bought me an "I will miss you" silver necklace! How romantic is that?

MarieCurieGirl to OccamsRazor: LOL, so what are you up to?

Now, why couldn't I say something, you know, romantic to Joe? I am such an idiot! Although not as much of an idiot as Dude Mann. He is now dancing around the bar area with Suit Lady, and I get a prickle at the back of my neck.

I glance sideways at William Brown, but he's not there. He must have gone to the bathroom. What if Dude Mann and Suit Lady get even crazier and someone gets hurt? I try to ignore them and concentrate on my instant messages instead. It's hard, because although I can't hear Dude Mann and Suit Lady on account of the earplugs, it's very unnerving to see them at the edge of my vision. Aren't the cabin crew supposed to intervene when passengers behave badly? Maybe *not* in first class.

Feminista to MarieCurieGirl: OMG! Kieran says where have U been 4 the last 2 weeks? Dude Mann is all over YouTube, Facebook & MySpace like a rash! He's ttlly buzzing—especially in America. He's the new teen phenomenon! He speaks to the disenfranchised, material youth.

MarieCurieGirl to Feminista: WHAT? You have *got* to be *kidding* me. How can he speak to the youth of America? He can barely speak at all! He's currently an accident waiting to happen!

OccamsRazor to MarieCurieGirl: BTW, thinking

of odd, ancient creatures, did you see the BBC article about the Amazon molly fish? Somehow it made me think of you. Here's the URL: http://news.bbc.co.uk/2/hi/uk_news/scotland/edinburgh_and_east/7360770.stm

I check out Joe's fish article and grin. Amazon molly fish, apparently, are all girls and have been all girls for the last 70,000 years. An evolutionary oddity. But does Joe mean that I am an oddity, or that he's already feeling like he hasn't kissed me for 70,000 years? Or that I'm just interested in biology?

Feminista to MarieCurieGirl: Kieran says Dude's signed a million $ deal 4 his life story & his upcoming part in the USA version of *The Flat.* Can U believe that?
MarieCurieGirl to Feminista: What? But he hasn't exactly lived for that long, yet. How can he have a life story to actually *tell*?
Feminista to MarieCurieGirl: Oh. I hadn't thought of that. Peaceflower says hi, BTW, she's sitting right beside me. We (Peaceflower, Joe, Brian, and me) are off to Hyde Park to hang. It's weird without U already. U don't mind us doing stuff together, do U? Although U're not missing much with Joe and Brian. Usual complicated sciencey chat stuff. Something about fish that don't make out.

I know it's completely irrational (usually I am definitely not the irrational type of person) but I feel a bit left out at the thought of them all going out together.

I know I've got my own exciting plans ahead of me, but I get a pang of longing to be with them. How can I feel homesick? I've only been gone for a few hours.

All of this is running through my mind as Dude Mann and Suit Lady lurch in my direction. The tingle at the back of my neck builds into a prickle, and I think, *Oh, no, here we go again.*

> **Feminista to MarieCurieGirl:** <3 ☺ on the romantic necklace!
>
> **MarieCurieGirl to OccamsRazor:** Have fun in the park. LOL on the fish. If I were them I'd really miss kissing you-know-who, even though I know fish don't really kiss. And I love my lovely romantic necklace so much that I may never take it off, sigh. In fact, I may never wash my neck!

Oh. My. God.

I should *never* instant message with two people at the same time, especially when I'm upset. I've sent Gina's message to Joe. What will he think? That I'm too needy, or that I'm moving too quickly?

The prickles at the back of my neck get even stronger, and I glance over at Dude Mann and Suit Lady as they crash into the seat of another passenger. Finally, one of the cabin crew asks them to stop, but they're pretty well ignoring her. How's a girl supposed to concentrate with all of this going on? I wish they would just STOP. *No, I don't wish anything. Really, I don't wish anything!* I tell myself.

As I am worrying that Joe will think I'm too intense,

because he's gone suspiciously quiet online, and as I'm also trying to stop the buildup of power in my brain, because Dude and Suit are way out of order, two things happen.

The first thing: All of a sudden Dude and Suit Lady stop lurching around and return to their seats like two meek little lambs. Did they finally decide to pay attention to the cabin crew? *Or is there another reason for their meekness?*

I turn my head and see William Brown standing by the entrance to first class. He is watching Dude and Suit Lady in a very intent way. When he notices me watching him watch Dude and Suit Lady his expression switches back to sphinx-like inscrutability.

As he takes his seat beside me, he shakes his head almost imperceptibly and says something to me. I take out the ear-plugs. "Are you okay, honey?" he repeats.

Instead of demanding an explanation for what just happened, I simply say, "It looks like we won't need these earplugs or the parachutes anymore."

The second thing: My computer beeps and I have an instant message from Joe.

Oh. My. God.

I blush and glance sideways at William Brown to see if he's noticed my beet-red face. He's reading some papers, so I sigh mentally with relief and refocus on Joe's message.

OccamsRazor to MarieCurieGirl: Agree completely on the fish—same feeling for me about you re: no kissing. ☺ Gotta go. Have a good trip. Love, You-Know-Who. XX.

Does that mean that he, you know, loves me loves me, or is he just using the generic "love" friends use all of the time? I think the latter, but long for the former, even though it's probably too early in our relationship to say "love." But a girl can daydream, can't she?

PROGRESS ON TRIP SO FAR

1. My new dad secretly compels people to stop when they are being a public nuisance. Surely a good use of ESP. It makes me very determined to master my ESP skills so that I, too, can be of future use to the general public.
2. My boyfriend is attempting to overcome his sciencey nature and returned mushy sentiment. Even though my message wasn't actually for him. Must practice at being more spontaneous and romantic.

Yay for progress.

Despite Dude, this is a *great* trip so far.

I wish that Mum were here to ask for advice. Or that Daphne Kat were here to cuddle with.

Although William Brown and I arrived on Wednesday evening and it's only Thursday afternoon, and I know I haven't been here long enough to, you know, get to know people, I'm already wishing I were home in our cozy London town house, instead of in this beautiful yet coldhearted mansion in New Jersey. I mean, it's lovely, but everything is either expensive or an antique, so I'm scared to actually *touch* anything!

And I haven't exactly had a warm reception from all of William Brown's "quirky" family.

When we came out of the airport into the wall of New Jersey July heat and sunshine yesterday to look for William Brown's chauffeur-driven car, I was *so* optimistic and euphoric, despite my jet lag. Then, when William Brown's chauffeur pulled up in a black Toyota Prius hybrid car to the standing bay at the front of the arrivals area to collect us, I totally approved of William Brown owning an environmentally friendly car. Another good sign.

"Darling," William Brown's beautiful, long-haired, blond chauffeur said as she leaped out of the Prius and threw her arms around his neck. "Did you have a good trip?" she asked in a very British voice. And just as I was thinking in my jet-lagged, fuzzy mind, *Goodness, the American way of doing things is very friendly, indeed,* the beautiful blond chauffeur kissed William Brown very soundly. *On the lips. And William Brown kissed her back.*

"Oh my God, it's so good to see you," he said, hugging her back. Then he kissed her *again.*

And as I was thinking, *Wow, they really are informal over here, and will I have to kiss everyone like that, too? And what great clothes chauffeurs wear,* because she looked really trendy and hip in bootleg jeans and a red tank layered over a longer white tank, she let Will go, took his hands in hers, and looked up into his face.

"I thought you were in L.A." Will beamed down at her. "But I'm thrilled you're not."

"I came back early so I gave your driver the night off," she said, then turned to me. "Oh, how rude of me, I just haven't seen Will for so long I'd nearly forgotten what he looked like. You must be Fiona," she said, smiling, and before I could even say hi back at her, she enfolded me in a big hug like we'd known each other forever. I noticed that she smelled great. Then I felt prickles at the back of my neck. "Of course you're Fiona, who else would you be? What a daft thing to say. I'm Jessica," she said, as she let me go. "Your dad's told me all about you."

I realized my mistake straightaway.

"Oh. You're his fiancée." Duh. My brain must have been really out there taking a vacation or something.

"You don't think all his female friends kiss him like that, do you?" Jessica teased me, smiling, and I blushed a bit. "They'd better not. Anyway, you both must be exhausted," she said as she opened the boot (which I'm told is called a "trunk" over here) and William Brown put our luggage into it. "Jump in, people, before airport security comes to tow the car."

I was in America. Jessica seemed lovely. Everything was wonderful and new. And instead of getting into the front of the car with Jessica (his Own True Love), William Brown climbed into the back with *me.* That made me feel so warm and fuzzy.

"Fiona, keep your eyes peeled out the right side of the car," Jessica called over her shoulder as we drove down the New Jersey Turnpike. I could see Manhattan, there on the skyline, like a shining beacon. Manhattan!

"See that tall spire there?" Will said as he put one arm around me and pointed at the skyline with the other. "That's the Empire State Building, and the glittery, shorter one is the Chrysler spire." It was so much to take in.

As Will told me about other places we might go and see, I started to feel really sleepy. Then he was telling Jessica about Dude, and I just *had* to ask him about it. I remembered about discussing ESP with strangers being forbidden, but my foggy brain reminded me of the prickles I'd gotten when Jessica had hugged me. Of course! During one of our "getting to know you" sessions in London Will had told me that she has ESP skills, too.

"Um, on the plane, when Dude Mann was being very, well, boisterous. Did you really—?" I asked Will carefully, wrinkling my nose again.

Will gave me his sphinx smile again and squeezed my shoulder. "What I believe, Fiona, is that we should go through life doing as much good and as little harm to people as we can. Mostly, we should try not to interfere with other people at all, because good deeds can cause bad repercussions. But sometimes, just sometimes, it's necessary to do something very small for the good of all. Don't you think, Jess?"

"Certainly." She smiled at me in the rearview mirror.

"So, if someone was behaving badly," I said, instead, "and was threatening the whole of, say, the first-class passengers with their antics, then it might be the moral thing to do to calm them down?"

"Or they might just get the idea that they should calm down and listen to the cabin crew." Will didn't actually admit he'd used ESP, but he did imply it.

Then Jessica said, "Just like that time I persuaded the guy who ran into the back of the car to admit that it really was his fault for not paying attention, and that he should just hand over the details of his car insurance instead of driving off into the night."

I think I understood what she and Will were saying, though. That it's not right to tamper with someone's thoughts unless it's *necessary.* But that would leave other stuff a girl could do with ESP. Like maybe if I learned to teleport I could spend time in the USA plus not miss my friends back home? On second thought, that's a bad idea, because how could I explain being in two places at the same time?

Anyway, it was nearly seven o'clock in the evening by then, which was really midnight in England, so it was hardly surprising that I dozed off in the car. Will had to nudge me awake an hour later as Jessica drove the Prius down a long gravel driveway and pulled up in front of this huge mansion just as the sun began to set.

Grand and stately, it was just like you see in the movies—all colonial, and painted a lovely gleaming white, with pillars, and a big front veranda with pots of red and white geraniums, and hanging baskets with trailing blue and white lobelia. Will told me that a veranda is called a porch, or deck, in American speak. Plus, there was a huge, sparklingly blue swimming pool at the side of the house. This, I thought, was what America was all about. All clean, and big, and colorful. Like a dream!

Unfortunately, some of it's turning out to be more of a nightmare.

I got my first inkling that Grandmother Gloria wasn't the warmest person on the planet when she came out of the grand front door to meet us. She's very beautiful, tall and thin, with short, blond, curly hair. But she also seems very starchy. You know, stiff and formal, not the type of person to wear pajamas or sweats or jeans around the house. Or ever.

She didn't even *hug* Will. You'd think she'd give him a hug after not seeing him for a month, wouldn't you? I mean, she did seem pleased to see him. She *did* kiss him on both cheeks and ask him if he'd had a pleasant trip. Then she turned to Jessica and did the same.

Then, when Will introduced me, she offered her hand and said, "I'm pleased to meet you," in a tone of voice that kind of indicated she wasn't very pleased to meet me at all. Or maybe I was just misinterpreting, because she did smile at me. Well, it was more of a grimace, really, and it didn't quite reach her eyes. I thought that maybe she'd warm up to me, that maybe she just wasn't a demonstrative kind of person. Then she switched her attention back to Will as they walked toward the house.

Apparently, there was a problem with Grandfather Frederick getting more obsessed with his latest project and not looking after himself properly, and would Will speak to him about it? she asked as we followed them up the steps and into the grand hallway.

Jessica sighed and gave me an encouraging smile. "Take heart. Your grandmother can be a bit formal and a bit of a worrywart at times." Then she hugged me to her side and we followed them into the house. I could identify with the worrying part, at least.

The house really is like something off the TV. All light walls and polished dark wood, with a massive chandelier in the middle, and a huge, impressive set of stairs right in the center covered in rich, red carpet. And the number of doors! You could get lost here.

Grandmother Gloria and Will walked into this enormous living room with embossed wallpaper and expensive furniture that looked French and ornate. You know, the kind of furniture you'd expect Marie Antoinette to have. As I looked around at all the oil paintings, and Chinesey vases, and interesting *objets*, Grandmother Gloria told Will that he really should have a word with Claire (his sister) about charity beginning at home, and about my cousin's TV addiction, because she, Grandmother Gloria, had already raised one family and didn't see why she should have to bring up a second one. Plus, what was she supposed to do with *two* teenage girls for the whole of the summer?

Will made appropriate soothing noises, and Jessica added that teenage girls generally looked after themselves. Then, when I yawned, Will insisted on taking me down to the basement to meet Grandfather Rick (only Grandmother Gloria calls him Frederick) before I fell asleep on my feet. The basement is Grandfather Rick's laboratory—he's an inventor. Anyway, Grandfather Rick seems very nice, although somewhat absentminded. When he saw Will he put down his latest invention for using wind power to fuel a family home (I didn't have the heart to tell him that someone had already invented modern windmills), and he was all, "William, my boy, how are you?" and *he* hugged Will. When Will introduced me to him, he hugged me, too, but I don't know if he was really paying attention, because after he told me I looked a bit like Claire when she was younger, he filled us in on how the windmill would work.

I was really woozy because of the jet lag and didn't take it all in, but I was a bit disappointed not to meet the rest of my new family. Aunt Claire was out at some kind of charity thing, and my cousin Naomi (who is fifteen—Will hopes that we will become great friends) was due back on Thursday (today) from a visit in Florida with her father and his second wife, so I pretty much went to bed straightaway. Grandmother Gloria wasn't very happy about that.

"William, you do realize that I have postponed dinner to fit in with your travel plans, don't you?" she asked, raising her thin eyebrows with disapproval. "Anne has made your favorite dishes, too. And Jessica's, of course. You need to eat healthy meals."

"Thank you, Mother, I know you worry about our eating habits, but I did tell you not to wait for us," Will said firmly. "They always give you too much food on the plane."

"That's true, it's like one meal after another on intercontinental flights," Jessica said, shaking her head with a smile. "But I'm starving, Gloria, I reckon I could eat Will's and Fiona's share." How nice of Jessica to try and lighten the situation.

Will was even more firm with Grandmother Gloria when the three of us went upstairs and he found out she'd put me in the smallest bedroom at the back of the house.

"Really, Mother, you've had a week to sort this out," he said. It was the first time I'd ever heard him even slightly exasperated with anyone. Plus, it was the first time I'd seen him even frown. I had to cut Grandmother Gloria some slack, though—if Will only told her about me a week ago, she must still be in shock about it.

"William, you're not the only one with a busy life. I've been up to my neck with the running of this house, my ladies' club, your father's erratic behavior, and a million other things."

"I know, Mother, I know," Will said, pushing his hand through his hair, and I felt a bit sorry for him. "But surely you could have asked Anne to prepare another room? I'm sure Fiona would love the yellow room."

"Anne has many other duties, and this room was already prepared," Grandmother Gloria said a bit haughtily.

I felt like an interloper! I also felt that I had to smooth over the bad karma, because the last thing Will needed after his long trip was a falling out with his mother. I didn't want to cause a wedge between them on my first day here!

"I think this room is just fine," I told them both as I stifled another yawn. "Because it's still twice as big as my room back home in London. It's, um, very nice." It was very pink and frilly, too, and not *me* at all. But I just wanted to go to bed. "Did you design the decor yourself, Grandmother Gloria?" I added, to be friendly. See, when I told Mum that I was a bit nervous about meeting my new family, she said that to make people feel at ease, you should compliment them and show an interest in them. So I thought complimenting the decor would, you know, make Grandmother Gloria warm up to me a bit.

I'm not sure if it worked, because Grandmother Gloria and Will both looked at me for a moment like they'd forgotten that I was there, then he said, "We'll talk more later, Mother." He gave her this really calming, gentle smile, and you know what? She actually smiled back at him and said, "I'll get it all sorted out tomorrow."

I had to wonder if maybe Will was exuding love vibes or something, because Grandmother Gloria had done such an about-face. A complete 180-degree change. But before I could think that through properly, I yawned again, and my brain felt so fuzzy that I knew I needed to lie down really soon.

Grandmother Gloria said, "Sleep well, Fiona," and smiled/grimaced at me, too. Anyway, Will got me settled into my room, showed me where the bathroom was, found my pajamas and bathroom bag in my luggage, that kind of thing. And that's the last thing I remember, because five minutes later I was tucked up in bed. Without even brushing my teeth!

When I woke up half an hour ago at twelve thirty, the sun was streaming in through the sheer pink curtains. I got really excited about exploring my new surroundings, because everything looks better in the morning, so they say. And now that I've had a shower, and brushed my teeth, I decide that I am going to give Grandmother Gloria the benefit of the doubt. But first I need to find Will and get some breakfast, because my stomach is growling so loudly it's embarrassing.

The house is really quiet as I walk along the landing and down the grand stairs. And as I wonder where to begin my search for Will, a brusque voice startles me and I nearly trip and fall.

"Good *afternoon*, Fiona." It's Grandmother Gloria. She puts a peculiar disapproving emphasis on *afternoon* as she clasps her bony, ring-filled hands in front of her elegant cream silk sweater set and cream silk pants. She smiles her grimace smile, and I can't help it, I just can't. She reminds me instantly of a spindly, bony spider waiting to trap a fly in its web. I know this is unkind, and I try for a friendly smile in return.

"Good morning, um, afternoon, Grandmother Gloria. It must be the jet lag, making me so tired. Have you had a good day so far?"

"Yes, thank you." Her eyebrows go up a bit, as if she's startled that someone would ask. Then she says, "I'm sorry you didn't wake in time to join us for breakfast or lunch. William had to go to the office; he said he'd see you later. Anne will give you a light snack in the kitchen if you can't wait for dinner. Now, I have some important phone calls to make and e-mails to write. I hope you can entertain yourself without making a noise or breaking anything." Then she turns on her heel and strides off.

Is she unfriendly, or just not good around teenagers? I mean, I'm a stranger in a strange land, her own granddaughter, and couldn't she hear my stomach growling for more than a light snack? So much for the Will love vibes.

Fortunately for me, Anne, who is polishing the glass pieces in the hall cabinet, hears both my stomach *and* Grandmother Gloria. Once Grandmother Gloria's out of earshot she stops her polishing.

"You poor, starving chick," she says, clucking with disapproval. "Let me say we're all real glad that you and your dad found each other." She shakes my hand vigorously. "Come on, kid, let's get you to the kitchen and feed you. You must be ravenous after all that sleep."

"Um, if you tell me where the kitchen is I'd be glad to make some food for myself," I say, because I'm not used to other people running around after me. Plus, she probably has a lot of other things to do.

"Don't you worry about that," she says as we walk down the hall to the back of the house. "I need to get the vegetables for dinner started anyway."

Anne is one of those people who is small, and round, and motherly, and you just know you are going to like her straightaway, so this makes me feel a whole lot better. At least she and Jessica seem nice.

"I've been working for Will for the last ten years," Anne tells me as she slices huge wedges of bread, cheese, and ham, and pours me a glass of milk. "Don't let your grandma put you off. She's a bit fussy and just ain't fond of change."

I'm not sure about that, I think, as I look around the kitchen to get my bearings. I still can't imagine anybody actually calling Grandmother Gloria "Grandma."

"This is an amazing kitchen," I say instead, because it is. All huge, and light, with marble work surfaces, white gadgets, and chrome finish. In the middle of the room is a pine table with four chairs.

"Yeah. Will let me redo it exactly how I liked when he first bought this house," she explains as she puts my sandwich and milk on the table. And as I eat, Anne fills me in on a few things. Like what a great man Will is, and how the family can be a bit "quirky" (there's that word again) but they're all basically nice people. Even Grandmother Gloria, whose bark is, apparently, worse than her bite. I hope so. Then Anne insists on cutting some homemade brownie for me (which is astoundingly delicious and, as she points out, a little bit of chocolate is scientifically proven to be good for stress relief and lowering the blood pressure, which I definitely think I need), and we're just discussing the pros and cons of brownies instead of chocolate cake, when Grandmother Gloria comes into the kitchen and ruins it all.

"Fiona, dear, I really encourage you not to eat cakes or cookies," she says as she eyes my empty plate and glass and my disappearing brownie (I'm stuffing the rest into my mouth because I'm worried that she'll take it away from me). "Eating a lot of sugar products is not good for your waistline and can cause health problems in later life." Then she sighs deeply. I can't help thinking about spindly spiders again.

"But I haven't had anything else to eat today, which isn't good for my stomach's health," I say to Grandmother Gloria as nicely (but assertively) as I can. "I totally agree that it's not good to each too much junk food, and thank you for worrying about me," I add, to try to smooth things over. I don't want to alienate her, but I am the new, improved Fiona, who sticks up for herself. Then I attempt to smile.

Grandmother Gloria raises her eyebrows at me and gives me her stiff smile. You know, the one that doesn't reach her eyes.

"Well. I'm *sure* you know best, dear," she says, implying that I don't know best at all, but I ignore that. "But you can never be too thin."

"Oh." I don't want to be too argumentative on my first day, so I think I'd better let that comment slide until I know her better. Plus, I want to ask her about using the telephone to call Mum, and whether I can use her computer to send e-mails to my friends, because my laptop isn't keyed into the house wireless Internet network yet. Before I can do that, though, another, younger woman with a box rushes into the kitchen.

"Hi, everyone, I can't stay more than a minute—my friend's waiting for me in the car and we're late for the food bank drive," she says in one breath as she rummages through cupboards and fills the box with cans.

"Claire, Claire, remember, less haste more speed," Grandmother Gloria clucks disapprovingly. "And do you really have to wear that shapeless sack?" I think this is a bit unkind, but at least I know who the woman is. "What would the ladies from the club think if they saw you like that?"

Tall and thin like Grandmother Gloria, Aunt Claire is one of those women who still looks great, despite wearing the shapeless silk dress and no makeup, and having her blond hair scraped back behind her neck in a severe bun. And she must be kind if she does so much for charities.

"I don't care what the ladies from the club think, Mother," she says as she puts cans of caviar into the package. "It's not what's on the outside, but what's on the inside."

"You're such a pretty woman, Claire, it grieves me to see you this way," Grandmother Gloria adds, wringing her hands. Which makes me totally rethink her previous unkind remark about Aunt Claire's appearance. She is her mother, after all. She's bound to worry about her. Then she tsk-tsks and takes the cans of caviar out of the box. "Do you really think the homeless will appreciate the beluga caviar?"

"Oh." Claire stops her frantic can search. "I guess that might not be appropriate." And then she notices me. "Oh my God, I forgot what today was, you must be poor Fiona," she says, in a really pitying voice as she rushes across the kitchen, plonks her box on the table, and takes my hand in both of hers. "The circumstances of your birth," she continues, shaking her head.

At that point Grandmother Gloria heaves another loud sigh and leaves the room, and here I am wondering what on earth to say.

"Um, thank you."

"It's *so* hard to grow up without a father," she says. "A girl needs her dad." I can see by her expression that she's genuinely worried about my social and mental well-being. "It's not your fault that you grew up deprived in a single-parent family.

You mustn't let it make you feel bitter or unloved, because you have *us* now."

"Um, I'll try." I can't help smiling at her. I think it's very sweet of her to be so concerned about someone she's only just met. "And you don't need to worry about me—my mum's great."

"Very good," she says as she pats my hands. "Oh, I hate to desert you, but duty calls. I hope you'll forgive me if I hurry off. We'll talk more later."

Aunt Claire picks up the box of cans and practically runs to the door. But before she leaves, she turns around. "Poor Fiona." She sighs again. "Have you met your cousin Naomi yet?" And when I shake my head, she adds, "You should go upstairs and bond with her. Naomi's the product of a broken home, too. She'll understand your *pain*."

I don't want to disappoint her by telling her I'm not in pain. But I think the part about meeting Cousin Naomi sounds good. Maybe she'll be normal. I mean, watching TV is *completely* normal.

When Aunt Claire leaves, Anne tells me not to worry, Aunt Claire can be intense, but she's well-intentioned. I go in search of Naomi, after Anne tells me I'll probably find her in her bedroom, and where exactly that is, as well as where my new bedroom (the yellow room) is.

I can hear the TV through the closed door. Dude Mann's unmistakable voice, as he regales the interviewer with a story about how he nearly got deported when coming through immigration (I wish!) because he made a joke to the immigration officers. Apparently, he'd joked about belonging to a terrorist group, when all he'd meant was that he is a soccer fan and once nearly got arrested for being drunk and disorderly.

I knock on the door, thinking about how I am going to break the ice.

"Y—yes?" Naomi opens the door just a bit, peering at me rather anxiously. I can tell at once that she's related to Aunt Claire and Grandmother Gloria, because she's tall and blond like them, with great bone structure.

"Hi." I hold out my hand. "I'm your cousin Fiona."

"I—I—. Yes," she says breathlessly, not opening the door any wider. "It's nice to meet you," she adds, poking her hand around the door to shake mine, which I think is rather odd.

"Um, I wondered if you wanted to go for a swim." It's the first thing that pops into my mind, even though I am really exhausted by all this strangeness and meeting people and don't particularly feel like swimming. I'm just not used to traveling anymore, like I was during the Traveling Years (as I refer to them) when Mum was in a band. "We could, you know, get to know each other a bit."

"Oh. Well, I'm really busy right now," she wheezes in her breathless, nervous voice as Dude Mann tells the interviewer how his experience with the immigration officers has scarred him emotionally, and how he's going to send his therapy bills to the department. "I—I—just got back from my dad's in Florida, and I have so much catching up to do, I missed all the British Dude Mann episodes, because Dad doesn't have cable, so—I—I—I'll see you at dinner." It's odd, because it feels like she's getting stressed just talking to me. She glances back into the room (probably at the TV), before turning back to me. "Okay?"

"Okay."

"I—I—I. Okay." And then she smiles nervously and closes the door in my face.

I see what Aunt Claire means about Naomi being troubled by her parents' divorce.

As I retreat to my new bedroom, I wonder about this seemingly dysfunctional family and why Will hasn't, you know, fixed them with his ESP.

Also, what am I supposed to do for the rest of the day?

ASSESSMENT OF SITUATION

1. I have no Internet connectivity, therefore no contact with, oh, the rest of the world.
2. I have no phone, ditto contact, with the rest of the world.
3. I have no TV, ditto contact and knowledge of what's actually going on in the rest of the world.
4. Nobody here seems very interested in getting to know me.

So, on the whole, my assessment is not very good.

I hate it when I'm having a great dream (featuring Joe and kissing) and then I wake up just as it gets to the good part. I hate it even more when I open my eyes and have no idea where I am and leap out of bed in a really undignified way.

Oh. I'm in the yellow room, of course I am. Not the pink one. Waking up two days in a row and being in a strange room each time is very disconcerting. Then I notice that I'm fully dressed. I must have fallen asleep due to the jet lag. Or possibly boredom. And it's only five in the morning, so what am I supposed to do from now until breakfast?

The second thing I notice is that the bedside lamp is on, which is why I can see in the first place. The third thing is the plate of bagels wrapped in cellophane, some little pots of jams, and a jug of fruit juice on the little bureau under the window. Next to that is my laptop. It's switched on and there's a note on it.

Dear Fiona,

Sorry I didn't get to see you last night—you were so exhausted I didn't want to wake you up for dinner.

Your laptop's all set up on Wi-Fi, so you're good to go with e-mailing and IM-ing your friends—I'm guessing you might wake early after all that sleep.

Thought you might be hungry for first breakfast, so *bon appétit* and happy surfing!

Love, Will

PS. Second breakfast is at 7 sharp—don't forget that orientation day for boot camp is today.

How thoughtful and sweet was that of Will? And how funny. His reference to first and second breakfast is so hobbit-ish, but then he knows that some of my favorite books and movies are the Lord of the Rings ones.

I immediately log on to e-mail and see messages from Joe (2 of them) and Gina (1). I open Gina's first, because I want to save Joe's for last so I can concentrate on any good mushy stuff that might be in them.

To: "Fiona Blount" <MarieCurieGirl@bluesky.com>
From: "Gina Duffy" <Feminista@bluesky.com>
Subject: Roma. La Città Eterna!

You will never in your wildest dreams guess what happened while you were still en route to New Jersey. Dad saved Angie's life last week (Angie is short for

Angelina, because she's an Italian cat—minty name) and her humans were so grateful and thrilled (they're extremely rich) that they offered Dad the use of their *appartamento* (Italian for apartment) in *Roma* (Italian for Rome) for an entire two weeks!

Mum booked plane tix for all of us, and we're off this afternoon. Talk about a last-minute holiday! Don't know when you'll get this e-mail because of time differences and stuff, but I hope you don't mind that I've asked Peaceflower to come along. I would have asked you, obviously, but you're not here.

Write soon and let me know what you're up to, especially as far as wishes are concerned. Had any good ones lately? Got to go and pack now.
Later
XX
PS. Do you think Kieran will find someone else while I'm away?

I know it's really unreasonable of me, but I do feel a slight pang of jealousy at the thought of them all together in Rome. I quash it, because I should feel happy that Gina even has another friend to ask along—until recently she only had me, after all.

I e-mail Gina right back to tell her, no, it's clear from the way Kieran looks at her that he won't be losing interest any time soon, and then another thought occurs to me. If Gina is taking a friend, then her brother, Brian, will probably take a friend, too. That friend being Joe. I click on Joe's first e-mail.

To: "Fiona Blount" <MarieCurieGirl@bluesky.com>
From: "Joe Summers" <OccamsRazor@sciencenet.com>
Subject: Guess What I'm Doing This Summer!

Hey there, Marie Curie Girl,

You've probably heard all about it from Gina already, but we're off to Rome for two weeks. Imagine that.

Wish you could come, too, but you'll be too busy checking out Times Square to miss me (no, not really—at least I hope you won't).

Have fun doing your science thing—I want all the details (and don't accidentally blow up the lab).

Fish kisses,
Joe

I smile at the fish kisses bit. I mean, it's not conventionally romantic, fish kisses, but I know what he means. And then another thought occurs to me. It's all very well me giving Gina advice about her relationship, but what if Joe meets a hot Italian babe, a young Sophia Loren look-alike, and forgets all about me? I click on his second e-mail.

To: "Fiona Blount" <MarieCurieGirl@bluesky.com>
From: "Joe Summers" <OccamsRazor@sciencenet.com>
Subject: PS

Don't go falling for any handsome American nerd

types at science camp. You already have an English one. ☺

XX

I really should take my own advice, I think, as I type a quick response to Joe. I mean, he's getting quite good at this mushy stuff, even though it's in a roundabout kind of way. I glance at what I've written. Should I send it? Before I can change my mind I click the "send" key.

To: "Joe Summers" <OccamsRazor@sciencenet.com>

From: "Fiona Blount" <MarieCurieGirl@bluesky.com>

Subject: Re: PS

Don't go falling for any hot Italian babes in La Città Eterna, either—you already have a hot English one. ☺

XX

Joe is honorable. He is cute. He also has strong feelings for me. He bought me this necklace as a Sign of His Affection, I think, fingering my trilobite, which I have called Trilby. Naming an inanimate object is not rational, but a girl has to let go and be a bit irrational every now and then. Everything will be okay.

Oh. Joe's online!

Honestly, I don't know why I got myself all worried about hot Italian girls, I think, after two hours of instant messaging with Joe, when Jessica knocks on my door and peeks in. I can't believe we spent so much time just chatting about stupid stuff, like fish and the latest pictures from the two galaxies currently crashing together. But you can't talk about mushy stuff *all* of the time, now can you?

"Good morning, Fiona, breakfast is nearly ready. You don't want to be late on your first day."

"Okay," I call out to her as she leaves. I didn't realize Jessica was here at the house already. Actually, I don't know what her and Will's arrangements are. Does she live here, too?

And okay, so I also feel a bit bad that I'm not telling the absolute truth to Joe about "science" camp, because couples should be honest and open with each other, shouldn't they? But then again, it's good to have a few secrets.

It was nice, though, to be able to tell him that I'm a bit nervous about my first day, and how the people will be and such, and whether I would get on with them. Being a loyal boyfriend, Joe thought that they'd all like me instantly, although he totally understood where I was coming from because of my history. After all the moving around I've done in my life with Mum during the Traveling Years and all the new schools I've started over at in my life, I am really hesitant about, you know, being the New Person again, and getting up in front of everyone, because teachers always make the new kid get up and introduce themselves to everyone, and make them tell the class personal stuff about themselves, which I hate to do. You just never know what the kids are going to be like.

Then I pull myself together. I am the New, Improved Fiona!

"Fiona, you nearly ready, sweetie?" It's Will this time.

I take one last look at myself in the mirror. I look okay, I think. My hair's flippy and looks kind of cool, with the aid of that Toni and Guy gel that Gustav gave me when he restyled my hair. Also, I'm wearing the hipster khakis and my black T with the diamanté kitty face on the front that I got on a shopping trip with Mum. It's the outfit I wore on my first date with Joe, so I thought I'd wear it today, for luck. Not that I'm superstitious, but it can't hurt. Plus, it seems to be the same kind of outfit that American teens wear on TV, so maybe I'll blend right in at boot camp. I take a deep breath and grab my khaki backpack.

"You look great," Will says when I open the door.

"So do you." He's all tall and handsome and very official in a black suit, white shirt, and a gray tie. Then, because I'm worried I look a bit too informal, I add, "You're sure it's okay? I shouldn't wear something more like, you know, school uniformish or something?"

"Will you stop?" This is a rhetorical question. I know this because he smiles as he takes my arm, and we walk down the stairs and into the kitchen, where there is a delicious smell wafting from Jessica and the stove.

"Well, don't you look cute and ready to wow all those new friends you're going to make today!" Jessica expertly flips a pancake, and then adds it to a huge pile she's already made. I wonder why Jessica is making breakfast, and not Anne?

"Um, can I do something to help?"

"How nice of you to offer, but early mornings are my gig. Anne doesn't start until eight a.m., and I don't get to cook that often in this great kitchen, though it is one of my life passions. We usually order in when we're at either Will's or my apartment in Manhattan," Jessica adds.

That kind of answers part of my question about where she and Will live.

"You two sit. You need all the calories you can get inside you, Fiona, for the work you have ahead of you. It's going to be a busy day, all that mental power."

It's a relief that boot camp starts early, which means breakfast early, because that also means I get to have breakfast with just Jessica and Will, instead of later with Grandmother Gloria and the rest of the family. I know that I need to try harder with them, but yesterday was a bit discouraging.

"They're a nice crowd of people," Will tells me, referring to the espees. "Once we get there and Jess introduces you to everyone, you'll be fine. I wish I could stay with you, but I have to go into the Funktech office in Manhattan today."

"It's okay," I tell Will as we both sit at the pine table. I try to look confident and unconcerned. "I'm used to being the new person and sorting myself out." I can see that he has a lot on *his* mind because his forehead wrinkles.

"Don't you worry, either, Will." Jessica bustles over and places a knife, fork, and plate in front of each of us. "I'll be there to make sure everything's okay. He doesn't want to steal your thunder," she mock whispers to me. I must look perplexed, because she adds, "Will is a hero, a giant, in the espee community; he doesn't want to distract everyone by coming in."

"Jess, you're exaggerating." Is Will blushing? I think he is.

"Nonsense, you're a genius, the whole thing was your baby in the first place." Jessica ruffles his hair, which is sweet. And then something else registers in my brain.

"You're coming with me?" I ask Jessica. I have to say that does make me feel better.

"That's the plan," Jessica tells me as she sits at the pancake-free table, and I am wondering what we are going to eat.

Then, I nearly jump out of my skin as the plate of pancakes floats across the kitchen, as if by magic, and settles in the middle of the table!

"Show-off." Will grins, but I know he's only teasing her.

"So, one of your"—I pause and glance covertly around the kitchen—"powers is moving things with your mind?"

"Yes, that, and some more, er, interesting powers, but I'm sworn to secrecy because I don't want to spoil your orientation day." As I wonder what her interesting powers are, a container of something golden brown floats across the room and settles next to the pancakes. It's very unsettling, seeing ESP in action.

"I wish I could do that, too," I say. Because at least it would be a skill I could use. For instance, I could move Daphne Kat from London to America for comfort. Then again the cold from the transatlantic crossing and the time it might take probably wouldn't be a good thing for a cat.

"I'm one of the boot camp teachers," Jessica tells me. She is? That's reassuring. "Eat up before it gets cold," she says, indicating my plate. "You'll have me for focus and shielding once real classes begin next week."

We eat in silence for a few minutes, because the pancakes are delicious (I make a mental note to take some maple syrup back for Mum, too), and then Will looks toward the security box on the wall.

"Any moment now there's going to be a buzz," he tells us. And it's right then there is a buzzing noise.

"Now who's showing off?" Jessica teases him.

"That'll be Steve to let me know the car's outside." Will walks over to the security intercom box on the wall. "Thanks,

Steve, we'll be a few minutes." Then he grins at me. "No, I didn't get a precognitive flash. I asked Steve to bring the car around for this time of the morning." Then he winks at me.

Time to go.

As we climb into the car, I realize that I know hardly anything at all about ESP powers or my dad's apparent superhero status.

WHAT I KNOW ABOUT ESP SO FAR

List of ESP Abilities

1. Compulsion
2. Precognition
3. Mind Reading
4. Empathy/Pain Removal
5. Telekinesis
6. Teleportation
7. Transformation
8. Acute Hearing
9. Acute Sight
10. Acute Smell

I have developed compulsion and mild precognition, but I think it would be *über*ly magnificent if I could read people's minds, too. Of course, I wouldn't want to read their private, personal stuff, because I wouldn't like people picking *my* private, personal stuff out of *my* brain on a whim. I would only use it for really important things, like if someone told me I looked good in an outfit and really they thought I looked terrible.

It must suck if all you get is acute smell, though, because what use could that be? Unless you want to pursue a career as a sniffer dog, tracking drug smugglers or something. Acute hearing seems pretty lame, too. Acute sight might be nice, because seeing through walls could be supercool if, for example, you could see a bank robbery in progress and were able to help stop it.

Personally, I'd also really like to develop teleportation, since that would mean I could transport myself from one place to another, poof, in an instant.

Think about it. If I could teleport, it would mean that I wouldn't have to travel in vehicles that burn fossil fuels, which means I would kind of be saving the planet, one carbon footprint at a time!

And if I could develop all of those powers, I truly could become a superhero, just like Will.

I can't wait for boot camp.

Chapter 4

"You're making me blush, Jess. I didn't do that much," Will says as he drives us upstate on Route 17 to Esper Hall, and as Jessica regales me with tales of Will's herodom.

Will actually had Esper Hall built in the first place, along with his friend, partner, and drug-trial coparticipant, Douglas Freiman. All with money they made when they first started investing in the stock market. They also cofounded Esper, the secret ESP company, and set out to find people with the same secret ESP skills.

"He's so modest," Jessica confides to me in a girly fashion, and I giggle. "He's a bit of a James Bond, too."

"He is?" What does she mean?

"No, I'm not. Don't listen to any of that, honey. Jess is just biased because she loves me."

"Don't pay attention to him. Like I was saying earlier, he gets uncomfortable about taking credit for things, and methinks the gentleman doth protest too much. He's rescued a lot of people from tricky situations when their ESP powers have kicked in. There have been quite a few times when it was dangerous, too," Jessica adds.

"I had help," Will protests from the front seat.

"And he's kind," Jessica tells me with a cheeky grin. "He insists on helping and bringing into the fold every new espee."

"Okay, Fiona, have you still got those earplugs from the plane?" Will asks me. "I think I need them to stop my big head from exploding after all this praise." I can tell that he's not really upset because he's also grinning back at me in the rearview mirror.

And as we drive on, and Jessica and Will keep bantering about his achievements, I want to ask them, "Are we nearly there yet?" like a little kid, but bite my tongue. It's good to hear them like this, because it's clear how much they love each other.

I focus on all the new sights, because I haven't yet seen much of America and I don't want to forget a minute of it. Route 17 is a busy road, with huge stores, diners, fast-food joints, and psychic readers. The farther north we go, the more the road narrows and the landscape changes into forest. We're suddenly surrounded by trees, as if it is a different country in the blink of an eye.

"Okay, we're nearly there," Will calls back to me. "We need to tell you about the transition, so you know what's going on." Transition? What transition? I take a good look out of the window. The dirt track finishes just ahead, and I can't see anything except densely packed trees.

"In a minute you're going to get a really funny kind of feeling in your tummy and brain," Jessica says to me, twisting in her seat so that she's facing me from the front of the car. She takes one of my hands in hers. "It's the protective shield around Esper Hall and the grounds. You're going to think that you want to turn around and go back the way you came, but that's completely normal. You might even feel a bit sick."

"What do you mean?" I'm still peering through the trees trying to spot Esper Hall. All I can see are even more trees.

"The security system is a telepathic shield, reinforced with some very clever software," Will says. "The shield keeps out unwanted intruders and makes it easier for Esper to operate in privacy and seclusion."

"A clever piece of software that your dad helped develop, I might add," Jessica tells me. "But don't worry. It gets easier to penetrate the barrier as your ESP skills improve."

"Okay, this is it. You ready?" I wish I knew what I'm supposed to be ready for.

"Hold on to my hand and your tummy tightly," Jessica says, and it's then that it happens. Will puts his foot down on the accelerator *and heads straight for the trees.*

I want to turn back. I must turn back. I can't remember why we were going down this pointless little road, anyway. And we're going to crash!

"I want to go home," I say, and I know that there's something very wrong. I feel sick. If only I could turn around I would feel better. . . .

"Closing your eyes might help." Jessica's voice seems to come from such a far distance, but I squeeze my eyes shut and try to think clearly. *Esper Hall. That's where we're going. Try not to let your mind get fuddled,* I think. And then all of a sudden the fuzziness and nausea disappear. I feel absolutely fine again.

"That's it, we're through," Will calls from the front of the car. "Open your eyes, Fiona."

I open them and gasp.

The forest has completely disappeared!

Instead, we're in a grassy park, with a man-made lake and little clumps of trees. Ahead of me is a huge manor house, built in a very European style. The manor house is more like a castle, really, with turrets at each corner. If it weren't for the parking lot and cars at the side, I might think I'd stepped into a Harry Potter movie and was at Hogwarts! Except it's a smaller kind of Hogwarts, and gleaming and welcoming rather than gloomily menacing.

"The boot camp wing is on this side," Will tells me as he pulls the car around to the left of the house. "You see that entrance there?"

I can see people in the parking lot, parents waving good-bye, and some young people ranging from about fourteen to eighteen walking up the steps into the entrance Will indicates. I get a thrill in the pit of my stomach, because these are real, live, espee kids just like me.

"Time to get cracking." Jessica climbs out of the car.

I freeze.

Will opens the door for me, but I'm so nervous, my legs don't want to move. When he holds out his hand I grasp it like a lifeline and make myself step out. Also, I note that he's put on sunglasses.

"Part of his disguise," Jessica jokes. "He doesn't want to be noticed."

"No, it's just a cool *Men in Black* look I've got going on," Will tells her, then he turns to me. "Big hug for you," Will says, giving me a really big hug. "And a big hug for you." He gives Jessica one, too. "I need to slide out of here, so I'll see you girls later."

"See what I mean about not wanting to be noticed?" Jessica smiles at me.

By now everyone else has already gone inside except for a scary-looking Goth girl, who pauses on the front step and turns to the man just behind her. She has short, spiky, black hair and is wearing thick black eye makeup, black jeans, black boots, and a black tank with a skull and crossbones on the front. I remind myself that you should never judge someone by their appearance. . . .

"This is pointless," she tells the man. "I already did these classes—what good are they? I could be spending my time more efficiently by working on my game. I'm going to make millions from it. Don't you *want* me to become a teenage prodigy millionaire?"

"Honey," he reasons with her, "money isn't everything. You've got plenty of time to become a teenage prodigy—"

"Actually, I don't, Dad. I'm almost seventeen, which means I only have three more years of teenagerdom ahead of me—"

"You turned sixteen last month, that gives you four more years. If only you'd open your mind and concentrate, you'd get a better handle on your powers."

"Dad, I've got enough of a stupid handle on my stupid powers."

"If you had, you wouldn't be repeating boot camp. It's for your own safety, honey."

I get a bad feeling about this girl. She reminds me of Melissa Stevens, the popular bully at my regular school. At least, she used to be the popular girl until everyone got fed up with her antics and I stood up to her. Remembering how I overcame Melissa reassures me. I can deal with Goth Girl.

"Don't forget, I promised you that new computer if you get through it this time," Goth Girl's dad says. "All those fancy extras you wanted, including great graphics, to make it easier for you to work on your game? You have options to help you through, you know. Like Joss Graydon and Samantha Wilson. If only you'd agree to—"

"Dad, no! I won't have anyone messing with my mind."

What does she mean? What didn't she agree to? I don't want anyone messing with *my* mind, either.

Goth Girl sighs deeply, and then she notices me watching her. She rolls her eyes and shrugs. "Whatever. You don't need to come inside with me, *Daddy*, I'm not a baby. See you later." She runs up the steps and dumps something in the bin (which I must remember is called a trash can in America).

"Take care of April," her dad calls after her, and she barely pauses to answer.

"Yeah, whatever."

"That's Christina." Jessica sighs and shakes her head. "Such promising talent, if only she'd allow herself to relax and embrace it."

As we walk toward the entrance, I hope that *I* can relax and embrace *my* talent.

We walk up the steps, and there, on the wall, is a large, oval, pewter plaque, engraved with the following words:

BOOT CAMP REQUIREMENTS

PLEASE BRING AN OPEN MIND, KINDLY HUMANITARIANISM, LOGIC, CREATIVITY, AND IMAGINATION WITH YOU, BUT REMEMBER TO DEPOSIT ALL YOUR PREJUDICES AND PRECONCEPTIONS (IF YOU HAVE ANY) RIGHT HERE.

What a great slogan! This cheers me enormously, because I can do those things. Then I pause, because directly below the arrow is the trash can. I peer in out of curiosity to see what Goth Girl dumped in there. It's a large manila envelope.

"I'm guessing that's Christina's schedule and information pack." Jessica pulls it out of the trash can. "Yep. She's going to need this."

Jessica pushes open the door and I follow her into the hallway. Sitting at a desk labeled REGISTRATION is a small sparrowlike woman.

"Good morning, Jessica, how lovely to see you," she says, her face lighting up in a smile. Then she peers at me over the top of her half-rimmed glasses.

"Same to you, Miss Bird. I hope they're not working you too hard."

I am just thinking, *What an appropriate name,* when Miss Bird responds, "No more than usual. Oh, and you must be Will's secret long-lost daughter. What a thrill! I'm so excited to meet you," she twitters as she bops up and practically hops around the front of the desk.

"Um, thank you," I say as she holds out her hand to me.

"Such a romantic story, such drama—young love nipped in the bud, a secret baby who grows up without the love of a father, only to be reunited with him years later—just like in the books." She pumps my hand with surprising vigor, as the familiar electric jolt I get from touching a fellow espee moves down my spine. "Everyone's in the auditorium at the moment for the welcome orientation, straight down the hallway and first on the left, dear, you'll see the elevator. You know where to go, Jessica. Oh, and you'll need your welcome pack and schedule," she adds, handing me a manila packet. "I hope you don't mind, dear, everyone else except the newbies got their schedules at the end of the last camp session. You can't trust the mail," she continues, lowering her voice to a whisper. "You never know who might be spying on it. Okay, that covers it." Her voice is bright and cheerful again. "Run along, or you'll miss the fun. In fact, I'll run along right with you because I'm part of the fun."

Miss Bird certainly talks a lot, but she seems kind. She flits off down the corridor, like a sparrow hopping along the lawn.

"What fun?" I whisper to Jessica as we move down the hallway, trying to keep pace with Miss Bird. She's certainly fast for someone her age.

"You'll see in a minute," Jessica tells me with a grin. "As I said earlier, I don't want to spoil the surprise."

Miss Bird stops in front of a wall, on which there is a large brass lamp.

"What's she doing?" I whisper to Jessica.

"Just watch," Jessica whispers back.

Miss Bird twists the lamp forty-five degrees, and the wall shimmers.

"It's a—a—hidden lift! I mean elevator, because that's American for lift, isn't it?" I babble, because my day is going from strange to outstandingly weird. Although, really, I'm not sure what else I expected from a secret ESP camp.

"Hurry, hurry," Miss Bird chides us kindly as she hops into the elevator and presses a button. Jessica and I step in, the elevator doors close, and then we whoosh downward so quickly it feels like my stomach is following my body at a slower rate. For the second time today I feel sick.

After what seems like hours but in reality is only a few seconds, the elevator jerks to a stop, and the doors open on to another white corridor with numerous doors leading off it. We follow Miss Bird as she hops to the very last door at the end. She pushes it open, and we walk into a large, brightly lit conference room, with huge windows that look out on the gardens. How did they do that? I mean, we're underground. I don't know what I imagined boot camp to look like, but this wasn't it. I was kind of imagining log cabins in the woods or something.

"It's a safety precaution." Jessica laughs at my wide-open eyes. "We have to keep the visible building clear of all ESP stuff, just in case of unexpected visits, but why should being deep in the bowels of the earth keep us from having a lovely view of the grounds? It's another piece of software Will helped create."

There are about thirty other students in the room, all chatting and laughing.

"We have to keep the official part of the company legal. We'd have a hard time explaining all the funding that comes to Esper from Funktech and other organizations owned by espees otherwise, so aboveground Esper is a scientific research center. But belowground is where the real work gets done," Jessica adds.

"More than just boot camp?"

"All in good time. All in good time. Some of it is top secret." She taps the side of her nose.

There are four groups of chairs, placed in sections against the walls, all facing the center of the room.

"Positions, please," Miss Bird calls out, clapping her hands, and the students all move toward their seats. How do they know where they're supposed to be? What is *my* position?

"You need to go over there, with the freshmen." Jessica indicates a group of six kids assembling at the back left-hand side of the room. There is one free chair, between a wholesome-looking girl about my age, with golden, shoulder-length, curly hair and freckles, and Goth Girl, who is sitting on an end clearly trying to leave as much space as possible between her and the rest of the group.

"Go on, Fiona." Jessica gives me a little push.

My heart sinks a bit. I have to sit next to Goth Girl? She smirks as I take my place, but Farm Girl, as I want to label the other girl, gives me this huge, beaming smile. "Hey, I'm April. Are you new? I'm new, too. Isn't this, like, exciting?" Then she introduces me to the rest of the group, apart from Goth Girl, but I forget most of their names instantly.

"Um, hello," I say to them collectively, "I'm Fiona."

"Dudette, you're William Brown's British daughter. Cool," a young Johnny Depp look-alike tells me. I think his name is Zak. "My 'rents told me about him and you finding each other."

"Yer dad's a legend," another boy, Sean, adds in a strong Irish accent. About fifteen, he's a few inches taller than me, with straight, sandy hair that falls across his eyes. "'Tis a real inspiration—how he and Douglas Freiman set up Esper and began finding all the other people with ESP skills."

"I don't see what's so great about all this ESP stuff." Goth Girl shakes her head and smirks at us. "But it's kinda sweet to see you guys bonding over your espee superiority. You should totally become BFFs for life."

"That's Christina," April tells me, looking across at Goth Girl. "My cousin. Don't be fooled, she's a sweetheart on the inside."

"I saw that right away," Zak quips.

"Don't get any ideas," Goth Girl says to Zak. "My friends call me 'Eats Kids Like You for Breakfast.'" Goth Girl leans across me to bare her teeth at him. It's more funny than scary, actually.

"Really?" April's face is a picture of puzzlement. "I've never heard anybody calling you that." Then, the confusion disappears from her face and she's smiling again. "Oh, right, that's a joke. Ha ha, you don't look like the kind of person who would be a cannibal, in fact, you look like the kind of person who couldn't even eat meat, which you don't, because you're a vegetarian. Anyway," she adds, speaking to the rest of us, "my friends sometimes call me Ril, or plain April, but I don't really have a preference. Which do you prefer?" she asks me, and I don't know what to say. She reminds me quite a lot of Peaceflower, all sweet and naive.

Before anybody can say anything else, Miss Bird claps her hands again and is joined by Jessica and three other people—a tall, rangy, dusty-looking woman; a short, swarthy, bearded man with a potbelly; and a pale-looking, tall, thin woman with long dark hair. She kind of reminds me of Morticia from the Addams family.

"Good morning, everyone, welcome to boot camp," Miss Bird continues in her avianlike way. Then she goes on to introduce us new people, but she doesn't make us stand up or talk about ourselves, which is a relief. But she does add that I'm William Brown's daughter, and there's a lot of murmuring around the room when she says that, and a lot of eyes turn to me. My face gets hot, but I attempt a friendly smile.

"And now, let me introduce my colleagues for those of you who don't know them. This is Jessica Waterstone, who is mainly responsible for teaching focus and shielding, as well as the specialized classes for transformation and telekinesis. Cristobel Lantigue"—Miss Bird indicates the tall, rangy woman—"will teach ESP theory and will lead acute hearing, smell, and eyesight. Herbert Rafaelle," Miss Bird says, nodding to the short, stout man, "is responsible for compulsion and precognition. Madeline Markovy will lead empathy, healing, and acute senses." Miss Bird gestures to the Morticia teacher before continuing on. "I will lead teleportation and also precognition and compulsion. We all have our specialties, most of us have all of those skills but not in the same strengths, but we're all available for any questions or help you need with any form of ESP.

"All espees develop the main ESP skills of compulsion, telepathy, and telekinesis to some extent, although not everyone is as gifted in all of them as they are in the first one they developed." Miss Bird pauses as April puts up her arm and practically jumps up and down in her seat with eagerness. "Yes, dear?" Miss Bird asks kindly.

"Miss, if we're all going to develop mind-reading abilities, then why do we need secure networks to communicate with each other?"

That's a very smart question. There's more to April than meets the eye.

"You've raised a good point." Miss Bird nods approvingly. "Not everyone will develop strong enough telepathy to transmit or receive thoughts over long distances, so we have the secure networks to address that problem. Now, where was I? Oh, yes. Once your minds are open, your other senses will become sharpened, too. We'll split into groups shortly, and the juniors and seniors can go off to their respective projects, but before we do we have a tradition of putting on a little show for our new members."

A show? What kind of show?

I don't have to wait long to find out.

Madeline Markovy moves to the edge of the room, leaving the four other teachers in the center.

Miss Bird and Jessica simultaneously disappear, poof, like magic. Cristobel Lantigue and Herbert Rafaelle shimmer and become Miss Bird and Jessica, just as the real Miss Bird and Jessica reappear again, and the four of them move around, swapping places, so it's hard to tell who is really who.

"Oh my goodness. There are two of them. That's, like, amazing!" April grabs hold of my arm.

One each of the Miss Birds and Jessicas simultaneously disappear again, just as Cristobel Lantigue and Herbert Rafaelle shimmer back to their real selves, and then Miss Bird and Jessica reappear, but this time there are two Cristobel Lantigues and two Herbert Rafaelles.

This is so confusing! How will I ever know if someone is their real self or not?

The two Cristobel Lantigues clap their hands and step back. At this signal several students from each group, except ours, rise from their chairs and levitate themselves up and around the center of the room. It's like synchronized swimming, except for the lack of water.

As they cavort above our heads, several more students from each group stand and cross to us newbies, and I hold my breath.

"Do you have a pet?" the student in front of me asks. I nod, thinking automatically of Daphne Kat, but before I can say anything he grins. "Got it. Calico cat, Daphne Kat. Likes to chase pens and eat General Tso's Chicken."

Oh my God. He read my mind. Can he pluck out other thoughts, like about Joe?

"Don't worry," April whispers across to me. "He's just doing light mind reading—it's really bad manners to do a deep reading on somebody because it's rude to pick secrets out of somebody else's brain, don't you think? Except sometimes I slip and do it when I'm upset or emotional, you know what I mean?"

"I totally identify with that." I do. I mean, I once nearly turned the bully at my school into a mindless zombie. By accident, of course.

"I just kind of read people's thoughts without meaning to. That's why I'm here. Oh," she adds, raising a hand to her

mouth. "Sorry, sorry, I didn't mean to peek, I promise to keep my mouth shut about your near-zombification experience."

Before I can take in that April just read my mind, the student in front of Zak takes a deep breath through his nose.

"You ate oatmeal for breakfast, with orange juice, and don't worry about that stomachache, it's just indigestion." Zak grins and nods.

"Acute smell and sight," Sean says. "Those skills are a really great help if you're going into the medical profession."

The student in front of two more members of our group closes his eyes and clasps his hands in front of his chest. The girls stand up, turn toward each other, and curtsy. And a moment later are looking at each other wide-eyed in shock.

"Don't bother trying anything on me," Christina warns the student standing in front of her. "This is just so childish."

"Childish, is it?" the student asks her, then grins mischievously and looks into her eyes. Christina's elbow bends, and she's raising her hand to her mouth. She's really resisting—you can see the strain on her face as she grits her teeth—but finally she's defeated. Her thumb pops into her mouth and she begins to suck on it. "There's childish for you." The student winks at her.

Just when it seems like things can't get more bizarre, the students levitating around the room swoop down and grab the hands of the students who are not defying the laws of gravity—that is, *us*.

"Don't be scared," the older girl who takes my hands says to me. "I promise I won't let you fall."

Before I can tell her that I'm not so sure about this, we're flying around the room.

This is much more exciting than any other first day I've had!

Once things calm down, we're all encouraged to open our packs and see what's in store for us.

ESP RULES AND TAILORED BOOT CAMP SCHEDULE—F. Blount

Rules.

1. For personal security reasons, ESP must not be discussed with non-espees. Any accidental revelation must be reported immediately to an experienced espee.
2. ESP must not be deliberately used on other people anywhere outside Esper Hall. This applies to all levels of ESP student.
3. The only exception to rule #2 is in the case of an extreme, life-threatening emergency.
4. All unauthorized uses of ESP on other people should be reported to an advanced espee immediately.
5. Deliberate, willful uses of ESP on other people, especially where harm is intended, will be punished.

Schedule.

Monday through Thursday

Period 1. ESP Theory and Technologies

Period 2. Focus and Shielding

Fifteen-minute break.

Periods 3 and 4. Focus and Shielding. This will change to your own ESP specialties once you have mastered focus and shielding.

Lunch

Period 5. Focus and shielding. Same as Periods 3 and 4.

Period 6. Socializing and Practice

Fifteen-minute break.

Periods 7 and 8. Various. Will change from day to day as necessary.

On Fridays, boot camp finishes at lunchtime so only the morning schedule will be followed.

It seems that I won't be able to do anything else until I've mastered focus and shielding.

I can't *wait* for Monday morning, and boot camp proper, so that I can develop my superhero status more quickly.

I am the possessor of an extremely high ESP ability quotient! I'm in the top 2 percent. Along with Goth Girl Christina, which was a bit of a shock.

All us newbies had to be tested after orientation today, to estimate our powers. The actual test wasn't very difficult, it just involved measuring brain activity and a kind of ESP MRI scan to see which areas of our brains were activated when different emotions were triggered at different times.

The testers showed us cute pictures, like kitties and puppies (which made me joyful and happy), or poor third-world children (which made me sad and frustrated), or the pale blue dot photo taken of planet Earth by the *Voyager 1* spacecraft from a distance of about four billion miles away (I was overawed and humbled by the mystery and vastness of the universe).

Then they asked us questions along similar lines to the pictures, like, "How do you feel about world peace?" (desirable, obviously). I felt pretty sick, disgusted, and mad when they asked me about the situation in Darfur, I can tell you.

Anyway, Will called me on Jessica's cell phone as Dad's driver, Steve, drove us home from boot camp. (Jessica and I took this cool underground tunnel and surfaced on the other side of the shield—much less intense than driving through it—in what looked like a regular old car park. Steve pulled up only moments later, none the wiser about where we'd come from.) Will's up to his neck with a problem and he was concerned that he couldn't come home and spend the afternoon with me as per our plans. "No worries," I reassured him, being a bit careful what I said on account of Steve overhearing. "You corporate superheros have to do what you have to do. Do you get to wear a special outfit with a cape and tights?" Will thought that was hilarious.

Jessica thought that it was pretty hilarious, too. "You're going to fit right in around here," she told me as we pulled up the driveway to the house and parked behind another Prius. And then, "I can't come in today—I have a couple of things I need to clear off my desk so that I can be at boot camp all next week. Will you be okay?" She pulled a set of car keys out of her pocket and headed for the other car.

I told her it was fine, I was still a bit jet laggy (which is partly the truth but not the whole truth), so I'd probably slob around. I *am* still tired, but only in a brain kind of way. I feel a bit fidgety, actually, so I'm going to go for a swim.

Just as I am about to walk through the side door to the pool, Grandmother Gloria appears out of nowhere. Her blond spidery ways are starting to creep me out a bit. I mean, how did she know I was here?

"You certainly can't swim alone, Fiona," she says, wringing her hands and shaking her head. "House rules. It's dangerous. You might hit your head on the bottom and drown, and then what will I tell Will?"

She does have a point. It isn't advisable to swim alone, just in case of an accident. I'm kind of warmed by her concern. Maybe she's more interested in my well-being than I had imagined. Maybe she's one of those people who sees danger in *everything.*

"All of the staff members are too busy to babysit you, and besides, it's way too hot for you to be outside. You'll get sunburned. It ages the skin so and causes skin cancer," she tsk-tsks. "You must try to preserve your youth for as long as you can. I do wish William had thought about all of the details before inviting you over for a visit."

I wish he had, too.

"Okay," I say a bit too brightly. "I don't feel like swimming after all."

"Good, that's all settled. It *is* for the best."

Right, then, I think, *I'll go for a walk, instead.* Around the grounds *and* for a walk into Richford, the local town we drove through on our way to and from boot camp. But I don't want to say that to Grandmother Gloria in case she finds a reason for me not to go.

When I get to the gates they're locked, and Steve, the chauffeur-slash-security guard looks at me as if I am mad to want to go for a walk when the weather is nearing 100 degrees. "You need a car and driver to go out," he grumbles at me. Even when I explain that I just want to walk down the road to town and promise not to get lost or get heatstroke, and that I routinely don't get lost in London practically every day of my life, he just gets more growly and says that he'd better check with Grandmother Gloria to see what she thinks.

"It's way too dangerous," Grandmother Gloria's voice comes over the intercom a few seconds later. "Apart from the heat, and possible skin cancer and sunstroke, Will is a very important, rich man and we don't want you getting kidnapped."

I give up. I am formally renaming this house *Gulag* Brown. I'll speak with Will about my personal freedoms later. In the meantime, I'm going to go back to the house and ask Grandmother Gloria, nicely but firmly, about that phone call to Mum, since I don't have a mobile—I mean cell phone—and the only landline I noticed so far is in her office.

As I walk down the hall to her office I hear Grandmother Gloria's voice.

"Oh, Doreen, for all I know it's just a clever ruse to extort money from poor William!"

I don't mean to eavesdrop on her telephone conversation, I really don't, but her office door is slightly ajar and she's talking rather loudly. In fact, she sounds really upset. This could be important. Who is trying to extort money from Will?

"Can you believe it? That someone as intelligent and successful as my son could take that—that—grasping harlot's word for it without any evidence is totally inconceivable. This could be his *complete* ruination."

Grasping harlot? This is really *bad.* Poor Will! No wonder he's off at work sorting out the grasping harlot this afternoon, instead of here spending time with me. This problem he has is far more serious than I suspected. I know I should just leave and come back later, but this is my *father* Grandmother Gloria is talking about and I can't help it—I freeze right outside her office door. I have to know. Also, I'm getting prickles at the back of my neck, and not the good sort of prickles, either.

"Yes, I know, Doreen," Grandmother Gloria continues. "A simple DNA test *would* settle the matter, but William refuses. He insists that this girl's mother is telling the truth. How can he be sure? And even if it turns out to be true, what about all my hopes for him for the future? He's a responsible, caring member of the community, a great business entrepreneur, he could be the youngest president of the United States, and now this. The electorate will never forgive him for having an illegitimate child."

Oh.

You know that saying? That eavesdroppers never hear good of themselves? It certainly seems to be true in this case. My stomach twists into knots as I realize that the "grasping harlot" is Mum! And Will intends to run for president? I have ruined HIS ENTIRE LIFE! I should *never* have come here in the first place.

"Don't get me wrong, I don't want any harm to come to the girl. . . . Well, she *does* bear a slight resemblance to Claire when she was younger, but it's only slight. . . . Yes, I know that Will's a good man who takes responsibility for his mistakes, but have you thought about the implications? The ladies' club will expel me. And what'll happen to the rest of us if something happens to Will and he leaves his entire estate to her? We'll be thrown out on the street, penniless."

I definitely *don't* want Will for his money! Why would Grandmother Gloria think I would throw her out on the street, penniless? And how could she call me a mistake? To be fair, it wasn't like Mum intended to get pregnant. She *did* use protection. But she sometimes tells me that I'm her favorite mistake, just like the song by Sheryl Crow (whom Mum has met several times and is really nice), but Mum does it as a way of telling me how much she loves me and wouldn't want to be without me.

And Mum is a successful businesswoman, so it's not like *she* wants any of Will's vast money pie, either. She's got her own. Not anything like as much as Will has, but, as Mum says, how much does one person really need? It's true, Will did try to make Mum take a check for his share so far in my upbringing, which was sweet. He said to Mum that it wasn't supposed to be an insult to *her*, he just wanted to do the right thing because he hadn't even known about the right thing until now (on account of not knowing about my existence for fourteen years). Mum said that was very kind but she had more than enough money, anyway, and why didn't he put it in an investment account for me? I explained that I didn't want the money, either, but he was very insistent, and when I am old enough I am going to donate the whole lot to charity.

As all of this swirls around in my head, the prickles turn into a huge, big tingle.

If only I was back home with Mum. *I really want to go home!*

The tingle builds, it's roaring in my ears, and the rational voice in my mind is saying, *Oh, no, here we go* as the strange pressure builds in my brain, along with a thought. I REALLY WISH I WAS HOME. The pressure at the back of my head gets so fierce that I think I am going to explode! And although I do want to be home more than anything, it should be via the usual method of flight in an airplane and not via accidental teleporting. If teleporting is a skill that I can even perform.

But what if I accidentally have developed this skill and teleport myself BACK TO LONDON? How will I explain that to everyone? How will I get back here again? It will cause such a terrible fuss that the government will find me AND MY LIFE WILL BE OVER. And MUM'S LIFE WILL BE OVER. And WILL'S life will ALSO BE OVER, because people will put two and two together and make a trillion!

As my vision blurs I see the now-familiar spots behind my eyes, and a voice inside my head is screaming at me to STOP. I have to stop! I don't mean that I really want to teleport myself back home, because what if I really do it and can't re-teleport myself back again? The pressure is so intense I can hardly contain it, so what do I do?

I look around the hall, wildly, for something, anything. What can I do with the power in my head? I focus on the huge, floral, ornamental vase in the corner. I can't teleport myself, but I could try to teleport *that.* NO! Not teleport. MOVE. MOVE, because what if I teleport the vase and it ends up half in and half out of the wall or something?

MOVE THE VASE ACROSS THE HALLWAY, I think with all of my might. *MOVE THE VASE!* And I release the pressure in my brain.

The vase doesn't move across the hallway.

It flies at top speed, hits the opposite wall, and smashes to a million bits with a huge crash. Well, that worked out well. Not.

As I am wondering what to do, Grandmother Gloria pulls open her office door and sees me.

"Fiona, what on earth is going on? Are you all right? Did you hurt yourself?"

I'm kind of touched that her first thought is for my safety, but I am too busy trying not to (a) throw up, and (b) faint, because of the familiar nausea and head pounding, to answer her properly.

Then she spots the smashed vase. "Goodness. What have you done?" Her eyebrows knit together in frown.

"Sorry, I have to be sick," I mutter as I clamp my hand to my mouth and drag myself to the toilet to throw up. At least I remember where the toilet actually is, because throwing up on the expensive carpet would only be adding insult to injury.

What a mess I am in, I think five minutes later as I wash my hands and face and drink a little water to try to help settle my heaving stomach. What am I going to say to Grandmother Gloria? *Pull yourself together,* I think as I look at my pale reflection in the mirror. I'm going to have to face the music sooner or later, so it might as well be sooner. I take a deep breath and open the bathroom door.

Grandmother Gloria is waiting for me *right outside.*

"I'm sorry, I can replace it, the vase, I mean. I have the money," I babble. "From my stock market investments."

"What exploded?" Grandfather Rick asks as he comes up the basement stairs. One more person to witness my humiliation. But it must have made quite a loud noise if it even distracted Grandfather Rick.

"And if I don't have enough, Mum can help because she's got investments, too," I stress, because I don't want anybody to think that I don't pay my own way. Especially after overhearing Grandmother Gloria's conversation.

"She broke the Ming vase," Grandmother Gloria says, pointing at the pile of broken pottery, then she looks away a little uncomfortably, as if she's wondering if I overheard her conversation and is feeling guilty for what she said. "And now she's sick. It was probably fumes from science experiments. I told Will science camp was no place for girls," she adds quickly and examines her ring-covered hands instead of looking anyone in the eye.

Oh. My. God. The vase was a Ming? You know, as in the ceramics from the Chinese Ming dynasty, which ruled China from 1368 to 1644?

Panic hits me as I remember a news article I read online. A visitor tripped up and accidentally broke three Ming vases at the Fitzwilliam Museum in Cambridge. They were part of a $600,000 collection! Where on earth will I get *that* kind of money?

"Um, I was only just coming to ask you if I could phone my mother, and I felt nauseous and faint," I babble on. "I kind of stumbled and knocked the vase over. And I'm really, really sorry." This is obviously not the whole truth, but it's the best explanation I can come up with.

"Wow, that was some stumble," Naomi comments as she comes down the stairs. "I thought the house was under attack," she adds nervously. "You—you—must be super-strong." If only she knew, I think, as my misery increases.

"So has my other grandmother—got money, I mean." Wow, am I still talking? I can't stop. "She's a baroness—so please don't worry about me paying you back. I'll pay back every single penny." My head is pounding crazily.

"Gloria, it was a replica," Grandfather Rick says. "We can get you another one. Now, don't you worry, dear girl," he says to me, patting my arm, and I relax a bit. "I'm always stumbling into things and breaking them, so you have me to thank for that family trait." I feel even better then.

"It's just like Dude Mann on *The Flat,*" Naomi tells everyone, her eyes as wide as saucers as she looks from the pile of smashed Ming to me. "He didn't mean to drop all the plates on the floor when it was his turn to dry the dishes, you know, even though it *looked* like it was on purpose." I'm grateful for her support, I really am, but did she have to use such a bad example of an "accident" to try to vindicate me? I mean, it was totally obvious that Dude dropped those plates out of spite.

"You know," Grandfather Rick announces to us, "that gives me an idea for inventing a nonbreakable ceramic coating. Thank you, Fiona." He beams at me, then ambles back down to the basement.

"Er," Naomi says, looking from Grandmother Gloria to me. "Er, I'd better—" She motions vaguely upstairs toward her bedroom. "See you later," she mumbles, then leaves me alone with The Spider.

Grandmother Gloria doesn't say anything for what feels like an age, but is in reality only a few seconds. If there were a prize for making a person (me) feel bad without the other person (The Spider) opening her mouth, Grandmother Gloria would win.

"Perhaps you'd better go upstairs and lie down for a while, Fiona," she finally says. "If you're that sick then bed is probably the best—and safest—place for you."

I feel so miserable about everything. But on the bright side (if there is one) it would appear that I can move objects with my mind. . . .

"Oh," Grandmother Gloria calls after me. "Your mother called yesterday, but you were asleep. I'll send Anne up with the cordless phone."

I don't know what to make of Grandmother Gloria, I really don't.

So what is a girl to do when she's miserable but check her stock portfolio (Funktech shares are going up so I send a note to my stockbroker to buy more), and log on to e-mail?

To: "Fiona Blount" <MarieCurieGirl@bluesky.com>
From: "Jane Blount" <MusicProducer@sciencenet.com>
Subject: How are you?

Am a bit worried because I haven't heard from you. Called yesterday, and your grandmother said you were asleep due to jet lag. She sounded rather strict. You okay, or do you want to cash in the New York minute offer? Remember, rescue is on hand.

Off later to Somerset for the weekend (Mark surprised me with a minibreak), but will have my laptop to check e-mail (and possibly to book international rescue plane tickets).

All my love (and from Mark and Daphne Kat, too. She's missing you, hasn't stolen any pens since you left). Call me if you can.

Mum X

Before I can e-mail Mum back, there is a knock on the door, and it's Anne with the cordless phone with Mum already on the other end.

"Hey there, Fabulous Fiona, I was beginning to think you'd fallen off the face of the planet," she says. She sounds so close, even though she's 3,000 miles away.

"Sorry, Mum, I've been sleeping a lot and getting over jet lag and such, and I don't know if there's another phone in the house apart from the one in Grandmother Gloria's office," I tell her. "I still need to have a proper explore."

"Is she being difficult with you about it?" Trust Mum to get to the crux of the problem.

"No, no, she was just sending the phone up to me so I could call you. She's just a bit—well, rather like Grandmother Elizabeth, except even more fussy. Not very approachable, but not unkind. You know what I mean?"

"There's one in every family."

It's nice to just chat about this and that, and Mum tells me more about her minibreak with Mark. It's so romantic of him to surprise her like that.

"Anyway, darling, I hate to blow you off but I think that's Mark's car pulling up outside. Don't worry about Daphne

Kat—Sharon's popping in to see to her. I'll call you on Monday."

I feel much better after talking to Mum, but then I smack myself mentally. I forgot to tell her about the Ming Thing. I'll tell her Monday.

And then I open Joe's e-mail, which cheers me up even more.

To: "Fiona Blount" <MarieCurieGirl@bluesky.com>
From: "Joe Summers" <OccamsRazor@sciencenet.com>
Subject: Rome

Hey, Marie Curie Girl,

You're probably too busy hanging in the Village with a designer cappuccino this afternoon, or something equally trendy and New York-ish, but I thought I'd check in with you.

Flight was mundane, unlike some people's flights! Not a minor celeb, a glass of champagne, or a bite of sushi to be seen. (You posh thing, flying first class, unlike us plebs—I was squashed between Brian and Mr. Duffy like a sardine.) There was a slight incident in the Rome airport with my luggage—apparently it's gone on vacation to Las Vegas (how it managed to get on a flight for Las Vegas rather than Rome is a mystery. I just hope it doesn't get sucked into gambling away my jeans and T-shirts in the casinos, LOL) but I should get it in the next few days.

Apartment is right in the middle of Rome, which is handy for all the sightseeing we're planning. Also, we've already met the neighbors. Dr. Fiori is a paleontologist, can you believe it? Quantum mechanics is fascinating, but you know my true love is dinosaurs. So far I have to say the Italians are a friendly lot—Dr. F. and family took us on a quick minitour of the city, then out for dinner—how nice is that?

Anyway, lack of clean clothes aside (ugh, although Brian and Gina's mum says she'll pick up some emergency clothes for me tomorrow—you know how I hate shopping), I thought you'd like a little guided tour of our Roman trip so far so that you feel like you're here. Test your knowledge with this cryptic virtual tour of the Eternal City.

Before dinner (pasta, of course!) we wandered down the Via del Corso and were *aymayzed* by this legendary building where the founder of Rome, Romulus, was allegedly seized by an eagle when he died and flown off to be with the gods.

Next, down through the Piazza Venezia to the impressive building that received its more common name from a giant statue of Nero, then we retraced our steps to the biggest and most ambitious Baroque fountain in Rome.

Can you guess what these places are? I expect a full response when I get up in the morning. ☺

Tomorrow, we're off on the *Da Vinci Code* trail (Brian and I intend to debunk it)!

Sleep tight,
OR X

PS. You should definitely go to the Liberty Science Center, among other places. It has some fab new exhibits, from what I've seen on the Internet. Check out the URL below. Wish I were there. . . . (My luggage wishes it were there, too. . . .)
http://www.lsc.org
PPS. *Lo manco molto*

He must be missing me if he wishes he were here! And he's so thoughtful, checking out things for me to do in America even while he's in Italy! (I especially love the Italian bit, which I looked up on the Internet. It means "I lack very," which I think means he misses me.) I e-mail him back straightaway.

To: "Joe Summers" <OccamsRazor@sciencenet.com>
From: "Fiona Blount" <MarieCurieGirl@bluesky.com>
Subject: Re: Rome

Hi there, OccamsRazor,

I love the miniquiz—I can see Rome in my mind's eye! And to answer: the Pantheon, the Coliseum, and the Trevi Fountain! I await more questions. Do your worst.

New Jersey is really pretty, the house is fab, my family seems very nice (I just need to get to know them better). Lovely swimming pool and grounds. Living in the lap of luxury is *so* tiring, you know.

MCG X
PS. I miss you, too.

Okay, so I'm giving a rosy picture of my life here so far, but I haven't seen enough of it to give him more than first impressions. I think adding an X was okay, too. After all, he sent one to me. Oh, how I wish Daphne Kat were here so I could run all this stuff by her. She might be a cat, but you know, she's kind of spookily intelligent and she always makes me feel calm and collected. Before I go check out the Liberty Science Center website, I click on my e-mail from Gina to see what she's up to, too.

To: "Fiona Blount" <MarieCurieGirl@bluesky.com>
From: "Gina Duffy" <Feminista@bluesky.com>
Subject: Roma. La Città Eterna!

Buona sera, mia amica! (Italian for "good evening my 'girl' friend." I mean you're a girl and my friend, not that you're, you know, my *girl*friend, girlfriend! Isabella's teaching us some Italian words.)

Hope you're okay, and not having any more problems with wishes about the future or anything. Remember,

I'm here if you need me. Even though I am *migliaia delle miglia* (thousands of) miles away!

Anyway, here is a quick recap of our trip so far.
Apartment: *belissima!* (Italian for "beautiful.") All big and airy and very posh.
Roma: *molta belissima!* (Very beautiful!) Very Italian, which it would be on account of being in Italy.
Dinner at restaurant: *squisito tagliatelli* (delicious tagliatelli)
New friend: *Isabella, la ragazza molto bella* (the beautiful girl), who lives in the apartment next door. She's just like a fifteen-year-old version of Sophia Loren and really nice. She and her family took us on a quick overview tour of the city this afternoon. She knows the best places to go, and the best restaurants to eat in, and tomorrow she's coming with us on the *Da Vinci Code* tour!

I'll write more *domani* (tomorrow)!

Love and hugs (Peaceflower sends love and hugs, too—she still isn't convinced about using wireless Internet, she thinks it will scramble her brains!!!), and write back straightaway so that I know what you're up to.

Gina X☺X☺X☺

My boyfriend is in a beautiful city with a beautiful Italian girl.

Is she teaching him Italian, too?
Why didn't Joe mention her?
My post-Joe's-e-mail euphoria is officially destroyed.
But at least my portfolio has increased in value.
Maybe Joe will love me for my money.

"Okay, that's enough music for one evening. You need your beauty sleep," Grandmother Gloria announces as she turns off the CD player.

Bedtime? At ten p.m. on a Friday night? I'm fourteen, not four, for goodness' sake! Although it's true, I *am* still tired from the jet lag and boot camp orientation earlier.

I look across the living room at Naomi on the Marie Antoinette-ish chair, to ask her with my eyes if this is for real. But she either doesn't notice me or doesn't want to. She just gets up and says good night to Grandmother Gloria, and kisses her quite formally on her papery cheek.

I hope I don't have to kiss her, too. But I needn't worry, because Grandmother Gloria walks toward the door with Naomi following closely behind and says, "Good night, sleep well." Then Grandmother Gloria pauses and looks back to check on me, so I jump to attention. At least Grandmother

Gloria is an equal-opportunity early-to-bed torturer.

To be honest, I'm *glad* to be going to my room, because I can't seem to do anything right.

MY FAULTS ACCORDING TO GRANDMOTHER GLORIA (APART FROM BEING A MONEY-GRABBING DESTROYER OF MING VASES)

1. I don't wear the right kind of clothes. When I came down for dinner earlier, it was just Naomi, Grandmother Gloria, and myself, because Will was still at the office and Aunt Claire was out doing charity work. Grandfather Rick was a no-show because he was, presumably, perfecting his ceramic idea. Anyway, Grandmother Gloria took one look at me as I walked into the dining room and asked me if I had any formal clothes, because one should always make an effort for a family dinner. What is wrong with khaki pants and a plain white T? Personally, I think it's a shame that Naomi wears such drab clothes. They're very nice, but they are the kind of clothes that older women wear, not teenagers. Mum wears trendier clothes than Naomi. Still, I did feel a bit out of place at the formal dining table.
2. I eat too much. Grandmother Gloria didn't exactly say that, but come on, I need more than one square inch of grilled salmon and tagliatelli with a few lettuce leaves. I made each bite last forever to try to convince my stomach that it was getting more. Naomi just ate hers in silence. Rather quickly, as if she were ravenous, and I felt a bit sorry for her, so I asked if there was any more of this delicious salmon. Well, that launched Grandmother Gloria into a bit

of a lecture about how we should only eat what we need and not what we want, because did we want to be fat? Naomi blushed a bit at that, so I wondered if that was some kind of reference to the fact that she is normal sized and not wafer-thin like Grandmother Gloria and Aunt Claire.

3. I am in need of vast improvement. After dinner I was hoping to escape to my bedroom, but Grandmother Gloria had other ideas. After announcing that teenagers spend too much time online or watching TV, she "suggested" that we retire to the living room and read some educational literature. Naomi and I had to take turns reading from *A Guide to Good Manners* that I'm sure must date back to the 1950s, or the Dark Ages, because it was all about comportment, and sitting straight with your legs together, your hands on your lap, and being elegant and such, and not running around the house or causing a ruckus. Talk about boring! (But I did wonder if that last was a reference to my earlier accident.)
4. I listen to the wrong kind of music, which is apparently the problem with teenage culture today. I wanted to tell her that Mum listens to my kind of music, and she turned out really well, but I don't. Instead, Grandmother Gloria played us some serious classical music by Mozart, because, so she reasoned, he was a child prodigy and one of the most influential composers from the classical period. I didn't have the heart (or nerve) to tell her that as the daughter of a musician, even a pop-star one, I am familiar with a lot of the famous classical musicians, too, because Mum studies them for form and inspiration. It was quite good, I suppose, very boomy and full of wrath and ire in places, and

quiet and sad with lyrics about tears in other places. And to be honest I prefer something more gentle and happy, like *Clair de Lune* by Debussy. I didn't tell Grandmother Gloria that, either, because I didn't want to seem like a musical know-it-all. When Grandmother Gloria said it was Mozart's *Requiem* Mass (which I already knew) she looked across at me. Was she holding a requiem for her shattered Ming, or was it my imagination?

So when Will's car pulls up the drive just after midnight, I am lying in bed trying so hard to be calm and collected that I think I'm going to burst! I'm really worrying that I might get emotional and do something else by accident with ESP.

I even looked up some breathing exercises online earlier so that I could meditate. I mean, I'm not into Buddhism, I don't really believe that I'm Marie Curie reincarnated. (And why do people who believe they are reincarnated never say they were, oh, a shop assistant or a cleaner in their past life? There's nothing wrong with being a shop assistant or a cleaner, they're honest jobs, so why do people always claim they were someone famous?)

Ohm, I keep telling myself. *I am a calm pool of serenity and peace.*

But it doesn't work, because when there's a quiet knock on my door and Will asks softly, "Fiona, are you still awake?" I leap out of bed, which is very uncharacteristic of me because I'm usually so rational. Even more uncharacteristically, I launch myself across the room, pull the door open, throw my arms around him, and say, "I never meant to ruin all of your presidential hopes, and will never throw the family out on the street if anything happens to you, and maybe I *should* just go home and you can forget about me and maybe nobody will ever find out about me and your life will be back on track again."

Will pretty well assesses the situation immediately. He hugs me back tightly and closes the bedroom door as he ushers me inside. "You've clearly had an *interesting* day," he says. "What happened, sweetie? Was boot camp okay? Jess thought you'd had a good time when I spoke with her earlier."

The whole tale comes pouring out of me. How I think that Grandmother Gloria doesn't like me, doesn't believe I am really his daughter, and the Story of the Smashed Vase. I just can't seem to stop the words!

As I blather on and on he leads me across to my bed and sits us both down on it, all the while holding me. When I finally finish up with how I really don't want his money and that I will replace the vase and disappear from his life like a puff of smoke so that he can campaign in peace for the job of leader of the free world, he laughs softly and kisses the top of my head.

"Fiona, you are more important to me than any presidential campaign or stupid Ming-replica vase," he says quite solemnly. "I have you, and I wouldn't change it for the world. You're such an amazing, beautiful, caring person—and that president thing is all a figment of your grandmother's imagination. It ain't gonna happen!"

"You *don't* want to be president?" I am pretty shocked when he says that, because let's face it, a man with his kindness and special powers could really do his country a great service. He could do *humankind* a great service. But I am feeling very good about his perception of me. I'm amazing, beautiful, and caring? Well, I'm concerned about stuff, but I'm definitely not amazing or beautiful, but it shows Will's commitment to me as a father if he thinks those things.

"No," he tells me, smiling down at me, his kind brown eyes crinkling at the edges. "No way do I want to be POTUS. Or vice POTUS. I can do a great deal more if I'm working on the peripheral, you see. Out of public office."

I hadn't thought of that, but it makes perfect sense. I mean, if you were the president of the United States, your every move would be planned and scripted from the moment you woke to the moment you went to bed. What kind of life would that be?

"What about Grandmother Gloria?" I ask him, because I really think she's a lost cause.

"You know, there's a lot more to her than you might imagine," Will says, shaking his head. "I know she can be—difficult." He pauses and grins wryly. "But I guess her life didn't turn out how she planned it. My dad was an up-and-coming whiz-kid accountant, and Mother had high expectations for him. He had other ideas. He just wanted normal things—nice home, yearly vacations, putting his kids through college, that kind of thing."

"That sounds fine to me."

"It *is* fine." Will squeezes me. "But Mother wanted more. She saw him as the next JFK, but Dad doesn't do politics. He doesn't do ambition, either. He just wants to do the things he finds interesting and have a quiet life. Mother wants, or wanted, him to be a successful highflier. I guess he feels he's disappointed her."

"So she's switched her ambitions to you, instead?" That makes sense.

"Yeah." Will sighs. "That's kinda the flip side of making a lot of money. Since I bought this house for us all, she's been on a mission to become part of the higher social order. I wish she'd just relax and enjoy life, but she worries too much about what other people think."

"And then there's me turning up like a bad penny."

"No, no, no, honey. She just needs time to get used to you. Can you cut her some slack—for me?" Will gets up and paces the room. "I wasn't expecting the current problem at work." He looks so weary. "I should *be* here. With the family. With *you*."

I think that he really is a hero! He cares so much about everybody.

"I think I understand now," I say solemnly, because it all falls into place like a jigsaw puzzle. "Grandmother Gloria forgets to enjoy what she does have, even though she has a lot. She focuses too much on what might have been or what could be, rather than on what is. Plus, she worries about people hurting themselves all of the time. And instead of enjoying his life Grandfather Rick invents useless stuff because *he* feels useless in Grandmother Gloria's eyes."

"I hadn't thought about it quite like that, but yes," Will says as he sits down next to me again. "You are one very perceptive cookie." He taps my nose with his finger and smiles at me.

I make up my mind right there and then to give Grandmother Gloria another chance and to get to know Grandfather Rick better.

"Um, what about Aunt Claire? I mean, she seems sweet, a bit distracted with charity work, and such. . . ."

Will laughs at that. "As I said, you are very perceptive. My sister, Claire, has had a bad time over the last couple of years, with the divorce, but she'll pull through it. She's a good-hearted woman."

Divorce *is* supposed to be one of the most stressful things that can happen to a person, after all. It's right up there with moving house (which she also had to do when she got divorced) and bereavement! I resolve to give Aunt Claire a proper chance, too. If she's ever around long enough, because she seems to spend all her time doing good deeds.

"It must be hard for Naomi, too," I say, and Will nods. "I mean, she's had a tough time, what with her parents splitting up and her father remarrying."

I *should* make more of an effort with Naomi. After all, I've only been here two days.

"I never intended to just dump you and run, you know, sweetie," Will reassures me. And then he pauses again, and I guess that he's weighing how much he should tell me about his problem at work.

"I know," I tell him in my best reasonable voice. "It must be a very serious problem for you to have to change all your plans without notice."

"It's not serious. Yet. But it could become that way. A girl in Los Angeles contacted me through the secret espee website. It's exciting to find a new espee, there are so few of us, but she's not sure about meeting up with an Esper representative."

"Oh, just like me when I first developed my powers?"

"Yeah. I can't blame her for being suspicious, but she's only twelve and she's talking about being able to teleport herself."

"So, you think she might cause problems for herself if she teleported by accident?"

"Exactly. Add into the mix that she's the daughter of somebody famous."

"She is? Are you allowed to tell me who?"

"We don't know; she's being very cagey about it. But the fact that her parent or parents are famous makes it more difficult. It means that one of them must have taken part in the same drug trial as me, but they haven't come forward, and we can't see any obvious record of them in the old clinic paperwork we have."

"Can't you ask the people who ran the trial? They might have better records."

"No." Will shakes his head. "They have no idea about the long-term effects. The first person to develop ESP skills was a year after the trial ended."

"Which is a good thing," I say, because it is. "I would imagine that if the company knew what its drug really could do, we'd all be in a secure government enclosure now." I should have thought about that before I opened my mouth in the first place. "Will," I add, as another, more intelligent thought occurs to me, "does everyone who develops ESP skills have some connection to the drug trial? You know, either they took part or are the children of the people who did?"

"As far as we know it doesn't happen naturally. The drug was initially designed to help people with Alzheimer's or senile dementia, but it failed. We can't let the drug company find out about our abilities, and suspicions would be raised if we asked too many questions. We make do with what we have and hope that we can find the other espees and teach them to control their powers before they draw attention to themselves."

All of this makes my problems seem very trivial.

"What will you do? How will you find her and her parents?"

"She's in touch, so that's good. Here's the thing," he says, squatting in front of me and taking my hands. "I need to go to the West Coast to deal with some of this myself. I feel a responsibility for each new espee, and I want to make her transition as easy as possible. Would you mind me doing that?"

"Of course you should go," I say immediately.

"I thought that's what you'd say." Will ruffles my hair. "I'll leave Monday, so let's make the most of the weekend. Jessica's coming over tomorrow. Any thoughts about what you'd like to do?"

"As a matter of fact, I do have an idea," I tell him, thinking of me and Will, and Jessica, one happy family at the Liberty Science Center. I really like Joe's suggestion.

"Now, you get some sleep, sweetie," he tells me, pulling back the covers. I climb in, and he tucks them around me. I know I'm a bit old to be tucked in, but I kind of like it.

"You, too," I say as he kisses my forehead and turns to leave.

"Oh, I almost forgot. I have something for you." He reaches into his pocket and pulls out a mobile phone and a little pamphlet that explains how it works. "It's set to make international calls, too, unlimited, so you can call whomever you like, whenever you like. I'm sorry I didn't get it to you earlier."

My own cell phone.

"My private cell phone number is programmed in already so that you can call me anytime you want. Oh, and one good thing about the Ming Thing," he says as he pauses at the door. "At least it shows that your powers are getting stronger."

That's a good thing? How, exactly, if I can't control them?

I now know *exactly* how my powers getting stronger is a *great* thing.

It came to me as I thought about Will and the love vibes thing just now. Because it's true, everybody does seem a lot happier when he's around. Even Grandmother Gloria. Like the other night, when we first arrived, Grandmother Gloria was grumbling about me and the bedroom situation, and then she suddenly turned all nice. I had my suspicions right from the beginning but forgot about them amid everything else.

It's happening again right now. All of the family is present for breakfast, including Jessica, who arrived from Manhattan earlier. Even Grandfather Rick, because Will went down to the basement to collect him. Grandmother Gloria is all, "Good morning, Fiona, did you sleep well?" and "Frederick, let Anne fill up your plate, you need to keep up your strength." Not a word about dieting, or being thin, or anything. Then, she flutters her eyelashes at him and smiles at the table at large.

Grandfather Rick takes that as a sign of encouragement and tells us all about his latest device for creating the perfect scrambled egg. He seems to have forgotten about his non-breakable ceramic invention, which is good, because the last thing I want is for the Ming Thing to be brought up again.

"So many people in the world don't get enough to eat," Aunt Claire burbles, but it doesn't seem like her heart's in it, because then she digs right into her breakfast and adds, "not that we should feel guilty about our good luck to get enough."

Even Naomi joins in the conversation, when Will asks her if she's done any more sketches, and did I know what a great designer she is?

"I'm not that great, Uncle Will," Naomi says. "I'm just an amateur, really." But you can see that she's happy he's interested, because her face lights up. "I just wish I could go to New York Fashion Week in the fall. I could use the inspiration."

It's nice to know she has more in her life than Dude Mann.

Then, Jessica really makes Naomi's day when she says, "That's not beyond the realm of possibility. I have a friend in the fashion industry. Just say the word and I'll get you some tickets, if you'd like to take a friend or two."

"That's a great idea," I say, because it is.

"Well, fashion is a—a bit—" Aunt Claire begins. But then it's almost as if she's forgotten what she intended to say (probably something to do with not all people in the world having enough clothes), because she smiles and says, instead, "I can't see it would do any harm. Okay, guys, I have to hurry," she adds, getting up. "I'm being picked up in a half hour. We're fund-raising to save the whales today."

Naomi is all smiles and excitement, but then her face falls a bit. "Thanks, Jessica, but I don't know who to invite to go with me." I feel sorry for her, because it's fairly clear that she doesn't have any friends. She seems to spend all of her time in her bedroom. I know what that feels like, not having any friends. Until recently, I only had Gina as a friend, because I was so determined to stay below everybody's radar.

"I'd love to go with you, Naomi." Jessica comes to her rescue.

I thought Grandmother Gloria would object on the grounds of it being dangerous, even if Jessica was going to be with her, but she nods and says, "That's a good plan, because we can't have you roaming around Manhattan by yourself. It's not safe."

I wander around London by myself all the time, and nobody worries about me being in danger. Which reminds me, I must check with Will about getting out of Gulag Brown when he's not around. . . .

"That's settled then," Will says, nodding approvingly.

See? Definitely ESP love vibes.

So here's my plan. Because Will has so much on his plate being a superhero-slash-James Bond, I am going to Follow in His Footsteps. In his absence, I am going to use my powers (once I can control them) to *fix the family.* As soon as I figure out how. Then maybe the world. Bit by bit, of course.

"What's everyone got planned for today? Jessica, Fiona, and I thought we'd go do something interesting."

"Oh, like, just the three of you?" Naomi asks, and she kind of looks sad again.

It occurs to me that William must be like a, you know, surrogate father for Naomi, and along *I* come and take up his time and attention. She must be feeling left out. It seems mean to exclude her, so I say no, of course not, we should all do something together.

"How about Six Flags? It's ages since we went, Uncle Will; it would be so cool. Six Flags is a megahuge theme park with awesome rides," Naomi tells me, between bites of egg. "You'll absolutely love it."

"Um, sounds great," I say, even though it doesn't sound great at all. At least Naomi is happy, and it's the first time I've heard her string so many words together! Maybe this could be my route to becoming friends with her and putting my budding plan into action.

"I wish you'd told me that you didn't like theme parks," Will says, looking quite concerned as we stand in line for a ride called Kingda Ka, a huge roller coaster that goes up and down practically vertically. My stomach feels iffy just looking at it. "Your first outing in America and it's something that you can't even take part in."

I feel a bit more sick at that, because Will seems to be reproaching me. I really hope I haven't upset him. But I'm glad that he waited until Naomi went to the loo before saying anything, because I'd really have hated for him to have done it in front of her.

"I don't mind," I stress. "It's not that I *don't* like them, it's more that they don't like *me.* And anyway, I enjoy watching people, you know, have fun." Lame!

"But you're supposed to be *part* of the having fun."

"We'll still have fun," Jessica jumps in, flashing Will a look that says, *Drop it, already.* Then she half grins, half grimaces. "I'm not so keen on theme parks, either."

"I didn't know that about you." Will throws up his hands in mock despair.

"A girl has to maintain some degree of mystery," Jessica tells him.

"You British gals—is this part of your culture, or what? Doing things you don't really like? You need to be more pushy."

"I can be pushy, mister." Jessica shoves him lightly. "Now, you and Naomi go and have fun on your scary ride. Fiona and I are going to have a ball looking 'round the shops and indulging ourselves in people watching and something chocolatey and delicious."

Jessica is really great. She knows a lot about the music industry, too, so while we inspect the shops we chat about the different artists Mum produces. Turns out Jessica's met Madonna a few times, just like Mum has, so we have that in common, too. And then we bond even more over a Frappuccino and chocolate cake with a discreet chat about ESP. So by the time Will and Naomi go on something Naomi describes as the ultimate ride, we're swapping accidental ESP moments as though we've known each other forever.

I tell her the one about where I accidentally compelled myself to confess to throwing chalk at Mr. Simpkins, my Theory of Knowledge teacher. I mean, it wasn't me at all, it was horrible Melissa Stevens, and I didn't want her to get away with making poor Gaynor the scapegoat. Back in those days I was too scared to stand up for myself.

"Once, not long after my ESP kicked in, I was walking outside Bloomingdale's," Jessica says as she breaks off a piece of cake with her fork. "There was this poor man selling *Street News*—that's a newspaper homeless people can sell to help themselves out of their situation."

"Like the *Big Issue* in England?"

"Exactly. Anyway, this rich-looking woman was about to go into Bloomingdale's, and the homeless man approached her to purchase a copy of the paper. She just looked down her nose at him and said he was the scum of the earth and that he was messing up the sidewalks of Manhattan. It made me so angry."

"What a horrible woman. What did you do?"

"Okay, I was a bit naughty." She grins at me. "I compelled her to empty her wallet and hand him her money—almost two hundred dollars! It was worth the nausea and headache."

"Way to go," I congratulate Jessica, and we high-five. What a *good* use for ESP.

"That doesn't mean you should just go around using your ESP whenever you want to," she cautions me, taking a sip of her Frappuccino. "But sometimes it feels good to redress the balance."

That sounds like an endorsement to me.

I am still thinking of this when Naomi and Will join us.

"The Twister was totally fab." An ecstatic Naomi flops into the seat next to me. "You really get twisted all over the place. You know, Fiona, if you don't like that kind of ride, how about something slower and more scenic? I was thinking, the Big Wheel is a fun way of seeing the safari park and all the grounds, and it doesn't jerk you around. Then you won't feel like you missed out. You, too, Jessica."

This is good, groundbreaking territory with Naomi.

"No pressure, you wimpy English gals," Will says with a grin.

"What do you think?" Jessica turns to me. "Are you going to let him get away with that?"

"Absolutely not. We Brits are made of sterner stuff than that."

A half hour later I am regretting my decision. The Big Wheel goes up fifteen stories and my stomach is not happy about that, but I am trying not to let my terror show. And as I am trying hard not to think about our dizzying height and to think instead about Naomi and how I can help her, something really odd happens.

Right at that moment I get tingles at the back of my neck!

Oh, no. What do they mean?

Then my brain flips to a kind of parallel universe, and I see this vision of Naomi.

I see her in a mall trying on lots of fashionable clothes in a size eight because she refuses to try on the size ten. She's alone and, of course, the clothes don't fit. The image flips and now I see her watching Dude Mann on *The Apartment.* He's getting married on this episode, and Naomi is heartbroken. I see her comfort-eating too many of Anne's brownies, among other stuff, and gaining a lot of weight. Now she's in an expensive store and slipping a silk scarf into her bag! As she tries to leave the store she's arrested for shoplifting! Poor Naomi, she didn't mean it, she was just unhappy.

The vision of Naomi in handcuffs with the security guard flips to another parallel. She still tries on the clothes, but instead of turning to a life of overeating and crime, she buys a lot of fashion magazines. She also buys artist's pads and pencils, and sketches lots more of her own designs for normal-sized girls. She's humming as she works, so I can tell that she's happy.

My ears are buzzing weirdly as our ride comes to a stop.

Was that a sign that my precognition is getting stronger? Is it giving me hints about how I might help her? Or was it just my mind diverting itself from being suspended so high up?

Although I try to make out that I'm fine in the car on the way home, I have to ask Will to pull over so that I can be sick.

Talk about embarrassing.

Naomi is very sweet about it and offers me some spearmint gum to take away the bad taste and settle my stomach. So you could say that my being sick helped break the ice a bit more.

The things I have to endure to become a superhero.

I am still puzzling things through on Sunday afternoon as I flip open my laptop. The strange vision thing didn't happen again today, even though we spent a lot of it together as a family, so maybe it was just my brain playing tricks on me.

Also, I am a bit concerned that I haven't had an e-mail from Joe or Gina since Friday. But as soon as my laptop boots up I see that Gina's online.

I am not going to say a word about Isabella and Joe. Instead, I will wait to see if Gina mentions anything, because I don't want to sound jealous or appear needy.

MarieCurieGirl to Feminista: Hey, Gina. *Come siete?*

I looked up the Italian for "How are you?" because I wanted to support Gina in her current commitment to learning the Italian language.

Feminista to MarieCurieGirl: Hi! *Va bene* (I'm doing good). *Come siete?*
MarieCurieGirl to Feminista: Oh, I'm doing fairly *bene*, too. Apart from smashing Grandmother Gloria's fake Ming vase (not a good first impression, I can tell you) and ruining WB's presidential aspirations because of being born out of wedlock. All the usual stuff.
Feminista to MarieCurieGirl: U're so funny!
MarieCurieGirl to Feminista: No, it's all true.
Feminista to MarieCurieGirl: Oh, dear. ☹ Is ur grandmother so horrible that she can't forgive U 4 the fake Ming? What's the rest of the family like? I'm worried about U!
MarieCurieGirl to Feminista: They're okay. Just a bit "quirky." On the plus side, when WB is around it's almost like he wishes for love vibes. Everyone seems much happier.
Feminista to MarieCurieGirl: U mean in a Corrupt-a-Wish kind of way? Granted, but they revert to normal when he's not around?
MarieCurieGirl to Feminista: Alas, that also seems to be true. And WB won't be around very much anymore, on account of having to go away on business tomorrow.
Feminista to MarieCurieGirl: That sux. U only just arrived!

MarieCurieGirl to Feminista: I know, but at least I had this weekend with him, and from tomorrow I'm going to be busy during the day with boot camp.

Feminista to MarieCurieGirl: Oh, BRB, Peaceflower's having a love crisis about Vespa Boy.

MarieCurieGirl to Feminista: Who is Vespa Boy and why is Peaceflower having a love crisis about him? You've only been in Italy 3 days! What about Buzz, the love of her life?

Oh. Joe's just come online! I will play it cool and not instant message him unless he instant messages me first. It's never good to seem too eager, is it? And I'm not going to ask about any beautiful Italians, unless he happens to mention them. One, in particular.

Two seconds later my computer beeps to tell me that Joe's sent me a message, and my heart leaps in my chest.

OccamsRazor to MarieCurieGirl: MCG! You're back online! I miss you, but it's been hectic around here. Dr. Fiori's got a great collection of fossils on loan from his university, and I got distracted. You know me. ☺. How was the Liberty Science Center yesterday?

MarieCurieGirl to OccamsRazor: Hi, you. Totally relate with the fossils. And we had a change of plan. We went to Six Flags, a theme park, instead. WB and I are saving the museum for another weekend.

OccamsRazor to MarieCurieGirl: But you hate theme parks. Remember that time you told me about when your mother took you to Euro Disney? Even the slow, kiddy rides made you barf.

MarieCurieGirl to OccamsRazor: I know, but I got to spend time shopping with Jessica. And I did actually go on a ride with Naomi, you know, just a gentle one so that we could bond more, right before we left the park.

OccamsRazor to MarieCurieGirl: You went on a ride??? You went shopping?? Who are you and what have you done with my girlfriend? ☺

Oh. My. God. He referred to me as his girlfriend. That must mean he really cares about me.

MarieCurieGirl to OccamsRazor: LOL. I'm Still Me, but sometimes you have to do stuff for family harmony.

OccamsRazor to MarieCurieGirl: Which is good, but you know, you can do things that you like, too, which *include* family harmony. It's your vacation, after all. You must assert yourself, Fiona. Remember how you revolutionized the school with the Fiona Phenomenon at the end of last term?

Joe's right. I mean, I did stand up to the school bully in front of the entire student body, which caused a lot of other people to stand up to her, too. But is that a recrimination from Joe? I bet Isabella is assertive. . . .

OccamsRazor to MarieCurieGirl: You still there?

Didn't mean to offend you. The pre-revolution you is great, too.

MarieCurieGirl to OccamsRazor: Aw, you flatterer. Anyway, today we had a lovely time swimming in our private pool and playing water games. WB's going to barbecue later. Total fun. How was the *Da Vinci Code* guided tour?

Feminista to MarieCurieGirl: I'm back! Vespa Boy is the boy on the Vespa who's been trailing us all around Rome. He fell in <3 with Peaceflower at 1st sight while she was throwing a coin in the Trevi Fountain, according to Isabella's translation. Peaceflower wanted my help writing a romantic poem about hearts and flowers for him. I told her he wouldn't understand because of not speaking English, but she said that their love transcends language. Oh, that reminds me. We took some pix yesterday on the *Da Vinci Code* tour. Isabella's picked out the best ones and I'm sending them as an e-mail attachment now. BTW, Isabella said U should invest in a company called Wilkon—she's really smart and invests in shares, too.

OccamsRazor to MarieCurieGirl: You posh thing, living in the lap of luxury. Debunking Da Vinci: magnificent! The guide was convinced that every word in the book is true, so Brian really wound him up when he said there was no evidence that Jesus and Mary Magdalene ever got married. By the time I pushed the guide about the Olympics not being created in honor of Aphrodite/Venus, I think he was

> ready to tear out his hair. But it was fun. Tomorrow, Brian and I are invited to visit Dr. Fiori's research center to check out his K-T boundary research—can't wait. I've got some pix to send you, set up for your amusement. One in particular is a puzzle for you. You'll know it when you see it. Can you guess what I'm thinking?

It seems odd that Isabella is concerned about my portfolio when she's never met me. I push that thought aside and open Joe's pictures first. It's the gang! Joe, Brian, Peaceflower, and Gina all making faces outside the different Roman landmarks. And there's Vespa Boy next to Peaceflower. I know it's Vespa Boy because he's sitting on a Vespa. It's pretty hard to see his face properly because he's wearing a helmet and his face is turned toward Peaceflower. He certainly acts like he loves her.

Oh, there's one of Joe by himself at the Trevi Fountain. His fingers are crossed, and he's about to launch a coin. Is this the photo he was talking about? Is he wishing for me to love him in return?

When I open Gina's pictures I forget about wishes and love. The first one features the gang at the Trevi Fountain again. Except this time a beautiful Italian girl, who must be Isabella, is sandwiched between Joe and Brian, but she's looking at Joe. It's pretty much the same for all the pictures—Isabella and Joe. They look so cute together, and it's almost like Isabella chose these particular photos to taunt me. . . .

OccamsRazor to MarieCurieGirl: What do you think? Did you guess?

Feminista to MarieCurieGirl: Isabella says to tell U hi. She feels like she almost knows U. She's really smart like U—U'd like her. Tomorrow she's taking Brian and Joe to her father's research center. Something about a kind of boundary to do with dinosaurs becoming extinct. U probably know what that is.

Isabella's going to the lab with Joe? She feels like she knows me? Why didn't Joe mention her to me? Why didn't *Joe's* pictures include her? Is he trying to hide something? I must keep my composure. I need to think about this.

MarieCurieGirl to OccamsRazor: No guesses. I have to go.

OccamsRazor to MarieCurieGirl: You okay? You sound a bit weird.

MarieCurieGirl to OccamsRazor: I'm fine, it's just that the barbecue's nearly ready and Grandmother Gloria has a thing about being late.

MarieCurieGirl to Feminista: Thanks for the pix. Will speak to you tomorrow.

It's not quite the truth. The barbecue won't be ready for a while. But I am wondering if Joe secretly wishes that Isabella was his girlfriend instead of me.

I am *so* not going to read anything into this.

I am also *so* not hungry.

HOT ITALIAN BABE, ISABELLA, VERSUS ORDINARY HALF BRITISH-HALF AMERICAN NON-BABE, ME

- HIB (Hot Italian Babe) has long, glossy, dark hair that curves around her face and shoulders like a shimmer of glamorous silk. I have brownish, shortish, cropped-to-neck-length hair that is spiky, flicky, and cute thanks to Mum's hairdresser, Gustav.
- HIB has large, almond-shaped brown eyes and long black eyelashes. I bet she never needs to use mascara. My eyes are just brown. Mum says that I have WB's eyes, which are brown and kind and twinkly, too; however, they do not feature extra-long lashes or any kind of resemblance to a nut.
- HIB is curvy in a very Jennifer Lopez kind of way. I am shortish and go in and out in the appropriate places, but could never be described as curvy.
- HIB has lips that pout naturally, like they're begging to be kissed. Mine are kind of bow-shaped but only collagen could make them look poutish.
- Not only is HIB very beautiful, she is also very clever. I am merely cuteish and, it seems, not as clever as I thought.

She was right about the Wilkon shares looking good, too. How can I possibly compete with such perfection?

Flying around the room, weird Naomi precognition moments, and Joe–Hot Italian Babe complications seem pretty normal compared to ESP theory.

Richard Feynman, Nobel Prize–winning physicist who was an expert in quantum mechanics, once said, "I think I can safely say that nobody understands quantum mechanics."

I think he was right.

And who knew that ESP theory could relate to string theory? I shouldn't be so surprised because they are both so odd and, frankly, mysterious. Although, the math for string theory is pretty convincing, so I'm going to have to trust the experts on ESP theory, too.

All pretty deep stuff to dive into on our first full day at boot camp.

"As some of you may already know, M theory demands eleven dimensions in total, apart from the regular four of left/

right, backward/forward, up/down, and space/time," Cristobel Lantigue tells us in her dry, dusty voice.

It's strange being in a classroom of only seven people. But then, not many people develop ESP, so I guess small class sizes are normal here. It's a fairly cozy room, painted a cream color like the others, with the same fake views of the grounds.

We're sitting in a semicircle, although Christina has pushed her chair away a little bit from the rest of us. Part of the not doing group stuff, I suppose. Come to think about it, Richard Feynman wasn't one for joining groups, either. The difference between him and Christina though (from what I've seen of Richard Feynman on YouTube) is that he was a kind, caring, pleasant kind of person, unlike Christina. What is *wrong* with her?

Zak, who is sandwiched between me and Christina, pushes his chair back a little so that he's nearer to her. When she gives him her scary scowl he shrugs and holds up his hands as if to say, "What?" He must be a glutton for punishment. April and I glance at each other, almost without thinking about it. Could it be a budding crush? Is he completely mad?

"I think he likes her," April whispers to me. Then, "I didn't know that science stuff. Did you know that?"

I half nod. M theory isn't something your average fourteen-year-old might know about in depth, unless she had a boyfriend with a keen interest in the laws of physics and math. The smile on my face slips a little as I remember that April is dangerous territory. I mean, she just plucked that thought about the zombification of Melissa right out of my head last Friday. I must be careful not to think about Joe, or the Hot Italian Babe. . . .

"Is this going to develop into a talk about sparticles and antimatter?" Christina breaks in, her voice dripping with boredom. "Because it's, like, so yawnworthy and this bunch of thickheads won't get it, anyway."

"How can you call the basis for the entire universe yawnworthy? That's sacrilege, dudette," Zak says as he looks at her in amazement. "I thought you were supposed to be smart."

"Christina, we're not all blessed with your grasp of difficult concepts and equations," Cristobel tells her. "Now, if you don't have a positive contribution to make, may I continue?"

"Sure. No skin off my nose." Why must she be so unpleasant?

"Thank you," Cristobel says, and then continues. "So, who knows what the four currently known energies of the universe are?"

I know what they are, but I don't want to appear like a nerdy know-it-all on my first day. I look around the semicircle, and apart from Christina, we're all looking at one another, as if to say, "Who's going first?" Nobody is putting up a hand. I glance across at Christina, and she smirks at me.

Zak raises his hand.

"Okay, I'm socially comfortable in strange, new situations. For the fair dudette on the *edge* of the group, I'll start the ball rolling," he says, looking pointedly at Christina. "Gravity is the obvious one." He states this so matter-of-factly, as if he discusses this kind of thing every day of the week. "People think it's incredibly powerful, but it's really weak. Some theoretical physicists think it's probably leaking out of our universe into another dimension, which is pretty spooky, don't you think? Or that it's leaking in, but either way could explain why it's so weak."

Obviously, Zak is very smart as well as being cutely Johnny Deppish. Christina's smirk slips into a scowl, but Zak just smiles at her, shakes his hands, and makes an "ouch" noise.

"Thank you, Zak, that's right." Cristobel nods.

"You're welcome," he says, flashing another grin at Christina. "See—it's possible to be a totally irresistible chick magnet and totally own quantum mechanics at the same time."

"It doesn't look like that from where I'm sitting." Christina folds her arms across her chest. "But it's your fantasy."

"Enough, people. Save the flirting for later," Cristobel says, and the whole class laughs. Except for Christina, who develops a sudden interest in her hands. "Okay, give me more. What are the other forces?" Cristobel encourages the group. "Anybody else?"

"Electromagnetism is the second obvious force, it's a thousand billion billion billion times stronger than gravity," Farah, one of the other girls, pipes up.

Mehreen, who is sitting next to her, jumps in straight afterward, "The last two forces are the strong force, which keeps particles together like glue, and the weak force, which is responsible for radiocarbon decay."

"What? Are you a double act or something?" Christina mocks.

"Ignore her, she's only mad because we just proved wrong her thickhead hypothesis," Zak says, smirking right back at Christina.

"It's *nice* to see you all taking an interest in the universe." Cristobel nods approvingly.

And now I'm really wondering how this is going to connect to using ESP. I mean, when are we getting to the good stuff? I'm anxious to begin practicing actual ESP instead of theorizing about it.

"Now, a big mistake all new espees make is that they draw power from within themselves exclusively," Cristobel continues. "That's what causes the nausea and vomiting. You use too much of your own power, instead of drawing power from the universe."

"Wait, we draw power from the entire universe? From other *people* and *animals*? Wouldn't that make us ESP *vampires*?" April says, grimacing with disgust.

I have to admit I don't like the idea of sucking power from other people, either. It sounds immoral.

"No, no," Cristobel Lantigue interrupts, as Farah and Mehreen say that they are equally sickened by the idea. "We take power from the universe at large. Never from other people. Imagine this: Gravity is the power you need to suck into your body from those other dimensions so that you can use your ESP. Electromagnetism is the force you're using to do that. While you're holding in your will, that's like the strong force gluing your power together. When you release your force, it's like the weak force causing decay. Is that clearer?"

"That kind of makes sense, but if gravity were any stronger than it is, if more leaked in, wouldn't the whole universe just implode?" Sean asks.

"Exactly. Exactly." Cristobel leans back against her desk and folds her arms across her chest. "I'm not saying that you are sucking in *actual* gravitons, but it helps to imagine it that way."

"I really don't get it." April's face screws up.

"Too much gravity. Too much power. It's obvious. Like you nerds, sucking in more ESP energy than you need, resulting in vomiting, blackouts, headaches, and who knows what else." Christina is smirking again. Then she pulls a finger across her neck and makes a croaking sound. "No more little espee. Haven't you ever heard of the Goldilocks hypothesis? You know, too hot, zappo, too cold, zappo, just right, bingo."

"We could die? From sucking in too much gravity? Like a black hole?" April squeaks.

"You sure like to scare people, don't you?" Zak chides Christina. "Why is that?"

"I prefer reality to fantasy."

"That's quite enough, thank you, Christina," Cristobel warns her. Then to April, "No, not quite like that. The point is that you need to make sure that you pull in just the right amount of power."

"I thought that ESP was to do with DNA and comes from within, which is why we need to eat so much to keep ourselves in equilibrium," Sean, the Irish boy, jumps in. "At least, that's how me mum explained it to me."

"That's right." Cristobel smiles. "But there's a limit to how much power we can use if we only use what's within us. Too much and we could damage our vital organs. Of course, this being the beginning of your training, you'll be focusing only on learning to control small amounts of power. Now"—Cristobel looks at April—"let me give you another example of how ESP theory ties into M theory. Imagine that when teleporting you are ungluing yourself using the weak force, moving your atoms from one place to another using the electromagnetic force to redirect your gravitons, the particles of gravity, then re-gluing yourself back together again with the strong force when you reach your destination. Electrons do it all of the time—disappear and reappear in different places."

That does sort of make sense. A weird kind of sense, but still sense.

"But you're using your own power to set things in motion—focus, gathering in power, carrying out an action, you're still burning a lot of calories. It causes cells to deteriorate, like the weak force decays carbon, and you have to be replenished by calories. Of course, you must not try any of this before you manage to shield.

"Speaking of shielding, that's enough theory for today, I think," Cristobel says right before the bell rings. "Study the handouts I've given you, try to grasp the basics. Jessica Waterstone will be with you in a few minutes. I suggest you take the time during socializing later today to get to know one another and bond. Your lives may depend on it." Cristobel gathers her large, battered briefcase. "Good luck with focus and shielding, group. Oh, and make sure you all take full advantage of the free high-energy bars and drinks out in the hallway. They're specially developed Esper products to help espees maintain equilibrium." With one last encouraging smile, Cristobel leaves the seven of us alone.

"That was pretty intense. What did she mean that our lives could depend on our bonding?" April asks the group at large. I was thinking the same thing.

"For when you're out on your secret Esper spy missions, idiot." Christina leans forward in her chair. "Why do you think they're so anxious to get us all to our maximum potential? How do you think Esper became so rich and powerful?"

"Dudette, what makes you think Esper is rich and powerful?" I'm glad Zak asked that because I want to know, too.

"Use your brain cells and think about it," Christina says, sneering. "You have a group of rich people, these Esper guys, all with powers the rest of humanity doesn't possess. You think they haven't got people in high places? In government? Running the richest companies in this country, possibly the world? Imagine how easy it is to steal research from another group if all you have to do is pluck it out of their brains, or how easy it would be to teleport into somebody's office and steal confidential files? And please stop calling me dudette."

"But my father is a man of principle," I jump in. "He would never do anything like that."

"And you've known him for how long, British?" The way she says British, *briddish,* sounds like an insult, but I let it pass.

"He is a very ethical person," I tell her, thinking of all the good stuff I know about him.

"He's known for his philanthropy," Zak backs me up. "He's a good dude. He was great dealing with all the confusion I caused when I first used my powers. And you know what?" He shakes his head at Christina. "There aren't enough espees to have that kind of control. How many kids did you see in the room on Friday? Maybe thirty? Do the math—that's nowhere near enough to rule the world."

"Maybe your dad *is* good." Christina ignores Zak and continues, "But don't assume that everyone with the same powers is gonna use them—philanthropically." The way Christina pauses on the last word makes me think. I mean, she's right. Who knows if everyone who took part in the drug trial is a good person or not?

"I wonder what the punishment is for using ESP willfully," April frets as she looks through her list of rules.

"Oh, it's bad," Christina, unhelpfully and totally expectedly, jumps in again.

"I just knew you were going to say that." Zak sighs. "After only one class I already know you so well."

"Take it from someone who's been through camp here at Esper once before, it can be really bad."

"Like what?" The rest of the group (apart from Zak) have very worried frowns on their faces.

"Like security bracelets that totally dampen your ability to use ESP. And there's no escape because those security bracelets are made using ESP technology. Once you have one on, you can never take it off, and Esper can track you via satellite. There's no place to hide."

"I think you'd have to do something really bad to qualify for that kind of treatment," Sean reassures us. "Like kill somebody, or something."

"Where do you get this stuff? You know what I think?" Zak leans right into Christina.

"No, and I don't care, but I know you're going to tell me." Christina leans right back, as if in challenge.

"Someone has been reading too many conspiracy theory thrillers." He leans even closer, and Christina backs off.

"You believe that if you like. Suckers." Christina slumps back in her chair, then laughs. "Just think how much money you could make as, say, an ESP assassin."

"Espees can make money without killing or stealing knowledge," I burst out. All this talk of espionage and murder is making me feel very creepy. The thought of harming another human being is against everything I stand for. "You know, on the stock exchange or something." Like me, except I don't make huge amounts because I don't have huge amounts to invest on account of only being fourteen.

"Yeah, come on," Zak urges Christina. "Chill. Life's too short and you're too cute to be so miserable. Let's get some positive vibes going about this instead."

"Positive vibes?"

"Yeah. Like, think of the good ESP can do. Like, what if ESP technology could be used for making advances in medical science? Our DNA is the same, but we've got a part activated in us that the rest of the world doesn't have. What if that's connected to, I dunno, illnesses like Alzheimer's? That's what the original drug trial was set up for, right? Or like, what if there were enough of us to persuade world leaders to concentrate on important stuff, like getting everybody fed and sharing resources?"

"Wouldn't that be against the rules?" April asks. "Making people do our will?"

"That takes us right back to what I was saying about good and bad people. Who are the good guys?" Christina is like a dog with a bone.

Zak, however, has a good point. I mean, wouldn't it be completely immoral *not* to use ESP in certain situations? Like helping Sir Bob Geldof really achieve his goal of making poverty history?

But before I can say that and before Christina can pour

down even more doom and gloom, Jessica walks into the classroom with two of the older students.

"Okay, people," she says as the students take their places at either side of the room. "Let's get some ground rules out of the way before we dive in. This is Jack and Serena; they're here for your safety. They're seniors—empaths and healers. Do you all know what their main abilities are?"

"They read feelings and can help with pain control?" April looks around at us to explain. "My dad's pretty strong on empathy. I always thought it was odd how he knew when I had a headache or had scraped my knee or something, and then he'd say he would kiss it better and the pain would go away; well, it always did. Now I know why."

"That's definitely part of their powers, April. But the reason they're here is that empathy healers are also able to shield others from ESP harm; you might say that they are the masters of shield building. Some of our adult espees are employed here specifically to help maintain and control the barrier that conceals Esper Hall. Our more experienced students help out as part of their training, as well as helping with boot camp newbies.

"You've just been covering the forces of nature with Ms. Lantigue, and how we think they relate to using ESP. Well, empaths can 'see' the flow of ESP powers. Also, they're like master keys. If one of you accidentally causes any kind of ESP harm to someone during class, they will be able to step in and undo whatever compulsion or mind-altering act you performed on another student. They also have the ability to sense the strength of ESP and can redirect the extra power if needed. So relax, you don't need to worry about hurting one another. Right, let's begin by placing you into teams of two so that we can get started on shielding," she says. "Whomever you pair up with, they will be your partner in this class for the whole of boot camp. You are going to learn to trust this person completely, because you are going to open up to them."

Jessica designates Sean and Zak as a team. Farah and Mehreen are another team. Which leaves April, me, and Christina, whom I'd rather not work with, but I feel bad excluding.

"Christina, April, Fiona, you can work together as a threesome, and I'll help out in between."

"That's great," April squeaks. "I *told* you we were going to be best friends."

"Okay," Jessica continues. "April, come and work with me for now for the first time so you can get an idea of how this should work. Everyone, I want you to take your partner's hands in yours and close your eyes. I want you to clear your minds of everything except for a bright pinpoint of light."

Christina and I look each other up and down. We have to hold hands?

"It's not like I have a transmittable disease, *Briddish*." She holds out her hands.

Okay, if she can do it so can I.

I think of my future possible superherodom.

Oh, the sacrifices one has to endure to save the world!

Ohm. I am a pool of serenity. Ohm. My mind is clear. Ohm. I am doing everything by the ESP book.

So why isn't this working?

I have Peaceflower's crystal in one hand, I have Trilby the trilobite in the other (for luck), and I am mentally constructing a circular wall around myself from the floor upward, just like Jessica explained earlier. As the wall reaches just over the top of my head it merges to become a semicircle that encloses me.

It's harder to do than when you're only building one part of the wall, which is why Jessica had us doing it in twos in class. But I may as well practice on my own, because that's the next step of the process, and I need to get ahead in this ESP business.

I'm only practicing picturing and maintaining my shield in my mind, I'm not actually attempting to harness my power.

See, Jessica says that we need to maintain our shields without thinking about them, and practicing like this will strengthen my ability to multitask.

Oh. My first phone call on my new phone!

My shield vanishes from my mind's eye as I pick up my phone.

"I have to assume that since you're answering your phone, your first day at camp didn't kill you," Will's voice greets me. "How'd it go? I want all the details."

"Oh, you know, same old, same old," I tell him nonchalantly. "A second-year girl managed to almost scare us all to death because she teleported herself part in and part out of our room," I add. It was *very* disconcerting to see her fingers wriggling through the wall like that.

"Ha ha ha. The joys of being a beginner."

"Not so joyful for me. I'm getting nowhere with this shielding stuff."

"Don't beat yourself up. It's only your first day."

"How on *earth* did you manage to work all this stuff out? You didn't even have a boot camp in your day."

"Well, let me see. How *did* I do it?" He's silent for a few seconds as he thinks it through. "It was all pretty much hit or miss in the beginning and took a lot longer to conquer without instruction. But I remember that studying meditation techniques helped me a lot."

"That's more or less what Jessica has us doing," I say. "In fact, I was just doing a bit of deep breathing and ohming."

"Fiona the smart cookie strikes again." Will laughs, and I'm warmed by his tone. "My advice would be to practice that, for now. Also, I remember that I would focus too much on putting my shield in place, and then if I switched gears to answer a question, I'd lose my concentration and it would fall. In the end I tricked myself into it—I thought of something completely different with the main part of my consciousness, and did the focus and shielding in the background. You could try that."

"I'm not sure what you mean." I frown.

"It's like when you're upset and you're trying not to use ESP dangerously. Take the Ming Thing the other day. You were trying hard not to think of teleporting yourself, so you thought about moving the vase instead."

"Yes, and that was really successful," I say drily.

"I don't mean you should go around smashing more innocent vases." Will laughs.

"I think I get what you mean. Maybe I should try to shield build while watching a movie?"

"That's the idea. But remember, no using ESP away from boot camp. Too risky. Just hold the picture of your shield in your mind."

"I will. Thanks for the tip. Did you have any success finding your new espee yet?" I ask.

"No, but I've only been here a couple hours—the flight takes almost as long as getting to London, even though it's the same country. I just got back from meeting with some colleagues, so I plan to check through the old records from the drug trial again. What are your plans for tonight?"

"Apart from trying to build a shield wall?"

"Why don't you take some time out? See what everybody else is doing. Spend some time with them."

Do I really have to?

"I might just do that," I tell him. After all, I did resolve to try harder, and if I'm going to help spread love vibes when he's not around, I need to know the family better. And then I remember about the whole personal freedoms thing. "Can I just ask, what can or can't I do in terms of leaving Gulag Brown?"

"Gulag Brown? It's not that bad, is it?"

"I was being ironic," I reassure him. "It's just that I wanted to go for a bit of an exploration on Friday and neither Steve nor Grandmother Gloria thought it would be a good idea for me to leave the grounds on account of heatstroke and kidnap attempts."

"Uh-oh. I'm so sorry, that's something I hadn't thought of. Okay, leave it to me. I'll speak with my mother about it. You can't get very far without a car, so I'll arrange for Steve to drive you if you want to go to the mall or something." Now he sounds worried, which wasn't what I wanted at all.

"Please don't worry about me," I hurry to say.

"Are you kidding me? You're the first person today that I *want* to worry about. I'll call you again tomorrow."

Five minutes later, tube of sunscreen in hand, I knock on Naomi's door. I have a plan.

I can hear Dude's dulcet tones so I know that she's watching TV. I am not hoping for any miracles on the getting-to-know-you front. But at least I can check that she hasn't suddenly started binge eating or something, as per part of my strange vision on Saturday.

"Hi," I say when she pokes her head around the door. "It's only me coming to see if you want to go for a swim or get a sandwich. Or both? Before it gets dark?"

"I—" She glances back into her room at her TV.

She's obviously going to turn me down. I sigh. I don't think a twenty-four-hour live feed of *The Apartment* is a good idea for anyone, especially if they're prone to becoming obsessed about Dude's possible future engagement.

"We don't have to do it for long," I say encouragingly. "You'd be back to the Adventures of Dude in no time, and you would be doing me a *huge* favor because I'm not allowed to swim alone."

"I—okay," she says rather breathlessly, after a few seconds' pause. "I'll just put on my swimsuit. I'll be down in five."

"I'll meet you outside with the sunscreen."

I head down the stairs. I'm going to use a new approach with Grandmother Gloria today. Instead of trying to do something and have her catch me in her spidery you-can't-do-that web, I'm going to just tell her what I'm planning on doing and why it's going to be *completely* safe.

As I get to the landing halfway around the staircase curve, I hear Grandmother Gloria and Grandfather Rick talking downstairs, and I pause.

"Frederick, why aren't you dressed?"

This is a bit worrying. *Surely Grandfather Rick isn't a secret nudist,* is my first thought.

"I *am* dressed. And may I add how lovely you look tonight? Are you going someplace nice?"

"I meant why aren't you in your tux? It's the dinner with partners at the ladies' club tonight, and as my partner, you're expected to *be* there."

"I am?"

"Yes. I told you about it weeks ago. *And* I reminded you this morning when you finally showed your face at breakfast. All this solitary confinement in the basement isn't good for you—you need to socialize more."

"Ah, Gloria, it slipped my mind. I had an idea, you see, for a device that could revolutionize trash degradability. I'm inventing a biodegradable can. What do you think? Do you want to come look at the prototype?"

"No, what I want is for you to go upstairs and get ready for the dinner."

"Aw, you know I hate those things. I never know what to say to these people—they're all so false and pumped up with self-importance."

I think it's a good idea if I don't make an appearance right now, so I stand silently against the wall of the landing. Grandmother Gloria doesn't say anything for what feels like an age, and I try not to breathe too loudly.

"Fine," she says at last. "I can see that I'm the only one in the family who's concerned about our standing in the community. Don't worry yourself about it for a second more," she tells him with a false yet ironic laugh. In that moment I feel sorry for her.

"Whatever you think is best, dear," Grandfather Rick says, totally not getting it. "I only came up to get a glass of water. I want to get a head start on this invention—it could really be big."

A few seconds later I hear Grandmother Gloria's office door close. I think it would be a good idea if I wait for a few minutes until I approach her.

"What are you doing?" Naomi appears at the top of the stairs.

I put my finger to my lips to shhh her, and she nods and silently comes to join me. I fill her in on the situation, whispering.

"That kind of thing happens *all* the time around here." She nods sagely. "You'll get used to it."

After we've guessed that enough time has passed for Grandmother Gloria not to wonder if she was overheard and for Grandfather Rick to go back down to his basement, we make our way to Grandmother Gloria's office. I glance at Naomi, who nods a bit hesitantly, so I knock.

"Yes?"

"Hi." I start in as soon as we're inside the door. "Gosh, you look lovely. Um, Naomi and I were planning on going for a swim. We'll stay together, of course, for safety," I say in a rush. "And for more safety, even though it's six in the evening and the sun is almost down, we've got sunscreen to protect against aging and skin cancer—see?" I hold up my tube of 40+ SPF. "And the exercise will do us good. We thought you'd approve of that."

Grandmother Gloria, expressionless, looks across at us. "It sounds like you've covered all the bases. That sounds fine."

For once she doesn't fuss on and on.

"That was very skillful," Naomi tells me as we walk down the hall and through the kitchen to the side door. "You really *did* think of everything first."

"Stick with me, kid." I grin at her. "I have a few tricks up my sleeve."

"What was skillful?" It's Aunt Claire. She's sorting through some bags of clothes on the kitchen table.

"Oh, just my handling of the sunscreen," I say, which is not a lie but is not the whole truth. I am actually *holding* the sunscreen in my hand. "We're off for a swim, Aunt Claire."

"That's wonderful. You girls should spend as much time together as you can. It's great that Naomi has a cousin to hang out with."

"Do you want to join us?" I ask, because Aunt Claire could do with letting her hair down a bit. "We're just going to splash about for a little while."

"Well—" She glances at the bag of clothes. "I'm not due to leave for another hour, maybe I could—"

"It would be great, Mom," Naomi says. "I haven't really seen you since I got back from Dad's."

"Oh, honey, I'll make it up to you," Aunt Claire says, then picks up a pile of T-shirts. Her expression turns sad. "So much to do, so little time; I have all these people depending on me. You girls go on without me."

That's a shame. For a moment I thought she was going to agree, but one small step at a time with the dysfunctional Brown family, I tell myself as Naomi and I walk to the pool. I think Naomi is hurt by her mother's absence.

"I totally blew it mentioning my dad," Naomi says as we reach the loungers and put our towels on them. "She hasn't gotten over him, even though it's been two years."

I don't know what to say, because I don't know her very well.

"Maybe she just needs more time?" I offer.

"Yeah. More time for her charities." Naomi dives into the pool before I can answer.

Everyone in Italy is probably asleep by now, but I check my e-mail before going to bed. I have e-mails from both Joe (2) and Gina (1). Yay. I wonder what the HIB has been up to, and whether or not there will be any mentions of her in either Joe's or Gina's messages. With trepidation, I open Joe's.

To: "Fiona Blount" <MarieCurieGirl@bluesky.com>
From: "Joe Summers" <OccamsRazor@sciencenet.com>
Subject: K-T Boundary

Hey, Marie Curie Girl,

How was science camp?

Dr. Fiori's lab is aymayzing. He's researching the decrease in oxygen in the early part of the Tertiary period after the K-T asteroid hit Earth. How carbon dioxide levels increased, creating the temporary greenhouse effect that wiped out most of the creatures on Earth and stuff. Brian and I are heading back there tomorrow and probably for the rest of the week if Dr. Fiori is okay with that.

So much for exploring an exciting foreign city, but then the science part is just as much fun. I guess it's the same for you attending science camp instead of touring Manhattan. Great minds think alike.

OR X

Just as I am thinking, *There's no mushy stuff (apart from the X),* I open Joe's second e-mail.

To: "Fiona Blount" <MarieCurieGirl@bluesky.com>
From: "Joe Summers" <OccamsRazor@sciencenet.com>
Subject: Don't Think You're Off the Hook

PS. You still haven't answered my question about what I was thinking at the Trevi Fountain. Can't you guess? Go on, I bet you can.

He still hasn't mentioned the Hot Italian Babe at all. Is that a good thing or a bad thing? I mean, Gina said the HIB was totally smart and into science, too. . . .

It takes me half an hour to think of a good response, because I'm attempting to be a non-jealous woman of mystery. Before I can second-guess myself anymore, I hit "send."

To: "Joe Summers" <OccamsRazor@sciencenet.com>
From: "Fiona Blount" <MarieCurieGirl@bluesky.com>
Subject: Re: Don't Think You're Off the Hook

<<OccamsRazor wrote: PS. You still haven't answered my question about what I was thinking at the Trevi Fountain. Can't you guess? Go on, I bet you can.>>

My guess: **私は愛すること愛する私を好みなさい**
Am I right?

LOL & XX

No, I didn't just learn to speak Japanese, but I thought it would be fun to use one of those online translators to give Joe something to work out. What I actually asked the translator for was: *that I love you like you love me* (hopeful thinking on my part). When you retranslate it back, though, the Japanese to English is totally not the same. . . .

Feeling pleased with my mysterious self, but also still worrying about the HIB and those photos of her and Joe, I open Gina's e-mail.

To: "Fiona Blount" <MarieCurieGirl@bluesky.com>
From: "Gina Duffy" <Feminista@bluesky.com>
Subject: Roma. La Città Eterna, Part II. Shopping!

Lots of fountains, lots of boutiques, lots of lovely sunglasses and purses. Click the pix to see Peaceflower and me in our new stuff! (Pictures courtesy of Vespa Boy, whose real name is Giovanni, which is Italian for John. It sounds much more romantic in Italian! ☺)

PS. How about some American pix?

Gina and Peaceflower are sunglasses twins. The frames of their 1950s-style sunglasses are bright yellow and hot pink, studded with diamanté, and they're holding matching purses on their arms. They're blowing me a kiss. They look so happy.

Then I notice something very obvious. She doesn't mention Isabella being with them. So where was the HIB? At the lab with Joe? I'm pretty happy when my new cell phone rings again, before I can jump to silly conclusions, and it's Mum.

"Fabulous Fiona!" Just the sound of her voice makes me homesick.

"Mum! I was going to call you when I got back from science camp, but it was already really late for you. It's"—I glance at my watch—"four thirty in the morning your time. What are you doing still up? How did you get my number?"

"Insomnia due to a new project to the first question, and second, Will called me earlier and gave it to me. How was science camp?"

"It was great," I tell her, feeling weird about the fact that I have to lie to Mum about camp. "We did quantum mechanics and stuff. It was even more fun than I thought it would be." There—both of those things are true. "How are Daphne Kat and Mark? Did you have a good minibreak? Is Daphne Kat eating properly?"

"Quantum sounds right up your street." Mum laughs, probably wondering (not for the first time) how she ended up with a science-loving daughter. "And Somerset was gorgeous, all green and lush in the summer sun. Glastonbury Town is a delight; we'll have to go there together when you get back. Daphne Kat is still eating like each meal is her last one. She *has* taken to sleeping exclusively on your bed. I think she misses you. *I* miss you. I especially miss our morning chats over breakfast."

"I do, too." There's a bit of a silence, because my throat is tight with homesickness. "Why don't we have that chat right now? What are your plans for tomorrow?"

She tells me that tomorrow she's working on producing a

CD with artist A (who is an absolute genius, as well as being a very nice person), followed by a late lunch with Sting to discuss an up-and-coming artist he thinks has a lot of potential, followed by an afternoon of dealing with difficult artist B, which will mean working late into the evening, then dinner in Hampstead with her ex-bandmates.

The Bliss Babes all had such a fabulous time when they got back together for a charity event Mum organized last month, they've decided to do the odd gig—maybe once every month or so—in small venues, just for the pleasure of making music.

As she chats away to me I remember the business of Grandmother Gloria and the Ming Thing.

"Mum, I need to tell you something. I had a bit of an accident when I first got here."

"Oh, do you mean the fake Ming episode? Don't worry a moment more about that, it's all in hand. Sharon's on the job—you know how efficient she is—and she should have a replacement sorted out by the end of the week."

That was quick. Then again, Sharon, Mum's assistant, is indispensible. But how did Mum know about it? Did Grandmother Gloria say something during one of Mum's attempts to get hold of me last week?

"How did you even *know* about it?"

"Will mentioned it when he called earlier."

"He did?"

"Of course, darling. He wanted to fill me in on things. I *am* your mother. It's such a shame that he's had to go away on business right at the beginning of your visit, especially as you're not having the best of times with the family."

This makes me feel even more fondly about Will. He called Mum to ensure I would be okay while he was away. How caring is that?

"Has your grandmother given you a lot of grief about the vase?" Mum asks, her voice all concerned.

"No. Not at all." This is true. I mean, she's not the warmest of people, but she hasn't mentioned it since Friday night.

"I expect Will thought you were worrying about it. He didn't want us to replace it, but of *course* we will, I told him. I insisted. Fortunately, he's totally in tune with wanting to pay one's own way in the world. Us Blount girls have our reputations to protect, don't we? So thoughtful of him to call to let me know you were okay," she says. "Anyway, darling, how are you getting on with the family now?"

"Better," I tell her. "Naomi and I went swimming together tonight, then we had dinner on the terrace. Burgers and fries, which was a bit naughty. Everybody else was out, so Anne, the housekeeper, said we should indulge ourselves a bit."

"Good to know that Naomi's friendly; I'd hate for you to be lonely. And there's nothing wrong with a bit of self-indulgence."

Then I tell Mum all about Naomi and how we had a good chat in the pool after the thing with Aunt Claire in the kitchen. About how Naomi gets on really well with her dad and his new wife, and she adores her twin baby brothers, but her mother can't seem to move past the divorce.

"It's almost like Naomi reminds Aunt Claire of her ex-husband," I say.

"That's so sad. I wish I could offer some sage advice, but I don't have any," Mum tells me, with a yawn.

"You should go to bed. You won't be fit to work tomorrow if you don't, sleepyhead."

After we say good night I check my e-mail one last time before bed. Should I e-mail Gina, all nonchalant, and ask about the HIB? Or would that be too obvious?

Oh. Somebody else either can't sleep or is up early. I have a reply from Joe.

To: "Fiona Blount" <MarieCurieGirl@bluesky.com>

From: "Joe Summers" <OccamsRazor@sciencenet.com>

Subject: Re: Re: Don't Think You're Off the Hook

<<MarieCurieGirl wrote: My guess: 私は愛すること愛する私を好みなさい Am I right?>>

"I loving like me who am loved"????

One for you, now: 崇拝される (I mean every word.)

XX

PS. Two can play at that game. ☺

PPS. Luggage no longer in Las Vegas but in Newark Airport. Maybe you could drop by and persuade it to come to Italy.

I laugh when I read the translation he got and even more

about the luggage. I load the Internet translator to see what he's replied back. Oh.

To: "Joe Summers" <OccamsRazor@sciencenet.com>

From: "Fiona Blount" <MarieCurieGirl@bluesky.com>

Subject: Re: Re: Re: Don't Think You're Off the Hook

<<OccamsRazor wrote: **崇拝される**>>

"It is worshipped"??

XX back at you

Worship is good, don't you think?

Chapter 10

ACHIEVEMENTS AND UTTER FAILURES SO FAR

1. Success in shield building: *zilch*. Considering the supposed strength of my ESP you'd think that I'd have made a breakthrough after four full days at boot camp, but no. Not even a glimmer. I don't have high hopes for day five, either.
2. Success with fixing dysfunctional family: *moderate*. Since our swim on Monday, Naomi and I have kind of fallen into a routine of doing that every evening. Only for a half hour, but it's progress. Aunt Claire is never around, so no progress there. Grandfather Rick still hiding in the basement, which makes it hard to evaluate him. As for Grandmother Gloria, she's a hard nut to crack, but I am determined not to give up.
3. Success in boyfriend flirtation: *excellent*. But only in Japanese. He still hasn't even mentioned the HIB, though. Should I be pleased about that . . . or worried?

As Jessica drives us to Esper Hall for the Friday morning session of boot camp, I stare out the window in silence. I'm beginning to understand Christina's point of view—that boot camp is a waste of time.

"Why so glum?" Jessica asks as the stores on Route 17 give way to forest. "You've barely said a word since I picked you up."

"Oh, you know, just the usual stuff."

"At home? I'm sorry. I really should arrange to be at the house more. It's just that I feel a little odd staying over when Will's away."

This is really nice of Jessica. But I can manage my problems myself. "Let me guess. Grandmother Gloria? I thought she liked you."

"She does, but after two years of dating the constant nagging about getting married and having babies can be a bit—wearisome."

"I can imagine." I grin at her, and at the same time I am thinking how weird it would be to have brothers or sisters. I'd practically be an aunt to them. "At least Will's coming home later today."

Jessica and I are going to JFK Airport later to collect Will. I feel bad that he still hasn't made progress with his missing espee, but I can't wait to see him. Speaking to him every day on the phone just isn't the same. Oh, how I wish I could make a breakthrough with ESP, just to make him proud. Then something occurs to me.

"Why don't you just teleport to L.A. and teleport back with Will? In fact, why don't you teleport us to boot camp every day? You drive out from Manhattan, collect me, then after camp you have to drop me home before driving all the way back. You'd save loads of time, and you'd really clean up your carbon footprint."

"Don't think it hasn't occurred to me," she says, laughing. "It's extremely tempting, but the rules are there for a purpose. If we get too used to using our powers all of the time, we risk discovery. Say for example Will teleported back and forth to L.A. He's quite high profile, the public face of Funktech, and what if he arrived at a meeting in L.A. five minutes after a meeting in Manhattan? It would look very odd. And we can't teleport to Esper Hall because of the security shield."

"I hadn't thought of it like that." I wonder if she's ever done it, though.

"Mind you, there are ways of managing more modest trips," she says, before I can ask her the question. "You don't really think I drive that far every day, do you?"

"You cheat?" She laughs at my shocked expression. "Go on, don't leave me in suspense. I want details."

"Okay, but not a word to anyone. I'm supposed to be setting a good example. When I drop you off I drive to a secure garage nearby. Then I teleport to a room in my apartment in Manhattan."

I'm glad Jessica's a bit of a rule breaker, because it just proves my point that some uses of ESP can be harmless.

"Hold on to your tum," she says as we approach the Esper Hall security barrier.

As we drive through it, I really hope that I can break through my own barrier this morning.

An hour later I am still trying, despite Jessica working solely with Christina and me this morning to help us break through our barriers.

"I'm never going to get the hang of this," I say, exhausted by the sheer effort of trying to concentrate and failing all week long.

By the end of Tuesday, Mehreen and Farah had conquered shielding and focus and improved so quickly in it that they graduated to their full boot camp schedule on Wednesday morning.

Lucky them.

By Thursday, Sean, Zak, and April had each made great strides with these skills, too, and were declared competent to move on to other lessons from then on. Which means that today, the class consists of only two people: Christina and me. Not an ideal situation. I'll have to spend *all* of the rest of boot camp with her at this rate.

It's a relief when the bell rings for the midmorning break. Time out to eat a lot of calories and rest. Which will be torture of one form, because everyone else will be talking about their most recent successes.

Everyone except Christina and me . . .

I almost wish that I could blame Christina for our lack of success teamwork-wise, but she's trying just as hard as I am.

"I told you it was pointless, Briddish. Aren't you wishing you'd listened sooner?"

"You want it as much as I do, Goth Girl," I remind her. "Although I guess it's just for the fancy computer your dad promised you, right? After all, you keep saying you don't actually care about any of this. But I think you're kidding yourself."

"Don't get any ideas," she says in her usual sneering

manner, but I don't think her heart's in it as much as it used to be.

I'm really great at *seeing* my shield, at picturing where it should be. I've even added details to it to, you know, give it substance and character. It's now a delicate green, with pictures of Daphne Kat, Marie Curie, Albert Einstein, and Joe around the sides (for inspiration), framed in silver. I also added a picture of the HIB with horns drawn on her head, just on the off chance that her presence would drive me to wrath and ire like that booming Mozart piece Grandmother Gloria made me listen to last week, but it's not doing me any good.

"You know, people with very strong ESP powers are particularly resistant to opening their minds precisely *because* of their strength of will," Jessica tells us.

"Mine is so resistant they may never kick in," Christina moans as she heads for the door. "This is my second time here. How many more times before I need to prove that it ain't gonna happen for me?"

I know how she feels.

I sigh and turn to leave, too, but then stop in my tracks at Jessica's next words.

"There is another way to get through this. It's a little—experimental."

Christina and I both turn back to her. This is *great* news, because at this point I'm ready to try *anything.*

"Really?" I ask eagerly.

"No way." Christina shakes her head. "I don't want anyone messing with my mind."

"What? You knew about the alternative and didn't say anything?" I remember back to orientation day when I first saw

Christina outside the entrance. Her dad said something about there being something that could help her get through. . . .

"Christina, I know you refused the treatment, but Fiona has the right to make up her own mind. It's new; it was only discovered in the last eighteen months," Jessica explains to me. "So far there haven't been any side effects, but it's only been carried out twice."

That sounds a bit ominous. I'm not sure I like that attempt rate.

"It involves mind merge," Jessica continues. "The basic idea is that we would help you relax enough so that you could open yourself up to an experienced empath, who'll scan you for the block, and help to break through it so that you can access your power. Then the empath will demonstrate to you, in your mind, how to build the shield and the basics of how to gather and release power, and how to direct it."

"Are there any drugs involved?" I ask, because I wouldn't be happy about that.

"Absolutely not." Jessica shakes her head. "The empath would use hypnosis to relax you, combined with a small amount of compulsion. The worst you would end up with, as far as we know, is a bad case of nausea and a headache afterward."

"As far as you *know*? Sounds like a fun party. Not," Christina grumbles. "I'm so not into this idea."

"What's another bout of nausea and one more headache?" I ask Christina. "At least it will give us a chance to be in control, so that we're not susceptible to accidental overuse of power with consequent nausea and headaches in the future."

"I love it when you use big words, Briddish." Christina rolls her eyes, but I can see that she's considering what I said. "It's more the 'as far as we know' part that has me concerned."

"It worked successfully with two of our current sophomore students last year." Jessica gathers her bag and papers. "Joss Graydon and Samantha Wilson. They were both seventeen at the time, and it was their third year as freshmen. You can imagine how frustrated *they* were. You could speak to them at break about it, if you want, to find out what it felt like for them. Of course, we'd all rather you came by your skills in the usual way, but I wouldn't suggest this if I thought it could cause harm. We'd need the consent of your parents, too, but only if you want to try."

"Okay, so maybe they didn't develop any side effects, but we'd still be, like, guinea pigs." Christina frowns. "Is that legal? Couldn't you get in trouble if we end up like cabbages?"

"Like all the rest of this is legal?" I ask her rhetorically. "I mean, ESP isn't exactly mainstream, accepted practice, is it?" Christina half grins at me, and I grin back. "And if those two sophomores are okay, then what are the odds that we'd not be okay, too, if we went ahead with this? They were the first guinea pigs, and scientific techniques can only get better after the first trial." Christina rolls her eyes at me, but I get the sense that she's not being disdainful, just playfully mocking me.

I think back to what April said on our first day. She was right—Christina's not as bad as she makes out. And I understand why she might be resentful and contemptuous of her peers. When you think about it it's only the flip side of how I used to be, before I trusted myself enough to be myself, instead of being scared to live my life.

"Well," I say, making my decision, "I'm game to try anything that helps me through the block. How about it, Goth Girl? You know what?" I taunt her, but in a good-natured kind of way. "If I get through this and you don't even try, you'll be spending the rest of boot camp by yourself. You'll have no one to insult, and that would be boring—plus, you'd lose all your sharp edges."

"I *would* kind of miss having you and the others to poke fun at."

"And by 'others,' you mean Zak?" I tease her, but Christina doesn't take the bait. "Or are you too much of a scaredy-cat?" I taunt, and it does the trick.

"Okay," she says. "Let's do it."

I did it!

I am now a person with a shield. Well, kind of.

It was just like Jessica said it would be. Miss Bird compelled me to feel relaxed, nearly to the point of being asleep, and then Madeline Markovy mind-melded with me. It was an odd sensation, kind of like having your mind taken over—almost like someone was rummaging through your drawers and cupboards.

I could feel a flutter against my brain, as if she were pushing open a window. It didn't want to open at first, so she nudged harder. "Relax," I could hear her saying in my mind. "Don't worry about a thing, just trust me." Her voice was so persuasive that I did.

After that, she opened and closed the window a few times, just so I'd remember where it was and how to do it myself. Madeline held the window open just a crack and pictured a large magnet in my brain. She pictured lots of little dots of light, which she said I should imagine are graviton particles, being drawn into the room that is my brain by the electromagnetism from the magnet. So many particles! Then, the particles formed a circle at the end of the magnet, held by the strong force. Then she said I should imagine the particles as a stream of fog, like when someone leaves the window open in the winter, and you can see the white of the evaporation from the heat inside.

That little bit of evaporation, the gravitons leaking outward, was my will being focused, she explained. It was being sucked outside by the cold. Open the window a bit more, and a bit more will gets sucked out. It sounded way too easy.

Of course, it wasn't that easy at all, because then I had to imagine a small, bright dot of light in front of the window, which would be a focus for my power. I really struggled with that, but when I asked her if I could imagine Peaceflower's crystal, instead, and would it be all right if I held it in my hand while I did this, because it had helped me during previous ESP moments, Madeline said that would be fine. She was kind enough to imagine it in my mind to take me through the steps.

She showed me the mist being sucked into the center of the mind crystal, and in my ears I could hear a really quiet whisper rather than the loud buzzing I usually get. Once the power was in the crystal, Madeline imagined a shield climbing around me (but without any of the embellishments I've added), and once it was completely closed, she released the power of the crystal on it.

It was a very strange feeling.

But I managed to do it for myself after only six attempts! Unfortunately, I can't maintain it for longer than a few seconds at a time. Madeline said I was using far too much graviton evaporation from my window—a lot of it was dissipating uselessly, which is a waste of energy—but that I was heading in the right direction. She did say that releasing additional power in this way was good, though, because sometimes people use too much for the task at hand, and this was how to release it safely.

Anyway, thank goodness it was successful for Christina, too. I didn't find out until I'd had my moderate success, because we had been placed in two separate rooms just in case we distracted each other.

Christina asked Madeline about using our newly opened will to do things other than shield-build, but Madeline told us that we had to take it one step at a time. Once we'd mastered holding a shield in place, then we'd learn how to multitask, because you need your shield in place for safety before attempting any other ESP actions. That way nobody could accidentally read your mind or practice compulsion on you.

Christina and I were both a bit headachy, but after we rested for a half hour and had a power bar and drink, we were ready to do more. Miss Bird said we shouldn't overdo it, but we should just join everybody else for the last period of the day, entitled, "Various. Will change from day to day as necessary," which today is a bit more socializing and practice. Why make us wait until Monday? It's just the seven of us, plus Jack and Serena, our empath/healers at the front of the room, in case we overextend ourselves or have an accident.

I don't understand why everybody's laughing at me, though.

"Love the shade of green." April smiles at me. "It's very restful on the mind's eye, so to speak. And the cute kitty picture. Is that your kitty back in London?"

Actually, they're not laughing just at me. They're laughing at Christina, too.

"Nice skulls, Goth Girl Dudette. Your mind is obviously a very interesting place," Zak tells her.

"Wait. You guys can actually *see* our walls?" I exclaim.

I turn to look at Christina, and sure enough, she's surrounded by a misty black bubble with skulls and crossbones all over it.

"Oh, yeah." Zak gives me a thumbs-up. "Good ones on the Marie Curie and Albert Einstein posters. Very cool dudes."

My concentration, and my wall, fall instantly.

"Don't worry," April tells us in between laughing bouts. "Nobody told us, either. It's a trick that gets played on every freshman. We're supposed to imagine an *invisible* wall. It's not a problem with normal people, but espees can see that kind of thing immediately, once they've grasped how shielding works."

We get the joke, and Christina and I laugh, too. Then April turns to me.

"Was that cute guy your boyfriend, Joe?" she asks innocently. "Oops, I didn't mean to peek into your mind. I kind of lost my concentration when your shield fell and accidentally read it. I'm sorry, I'm really sorry, I guess I was just so happy that you guys got to join us." Her face is crestfallen, and I'm quick to reassure her.

"Don't worry about it," I say, all the while thinking that I am definitely going to practice shielding hard to avoid accidental moments like this.

"You have a boyfriend, Briddish?" Christina asks me.

"Yes." I blush. "What's so unusual about that?"

"That's it? Just *yes*?" Christina puts a hand on her hip. "We need more details. You've been with us nearly a whole week and you didn't mention him."

"Can I listen, too?" Zak asks. "You know what Cristobel said, we have to bond. Our lives could depend on it." Then he flashes me a cheeky grin. "Tell me this at least, cuz I really need to know. Who's the hot dudette with the horns?"

I have to learn to share more. It's the American way. And it's not like Joe is a secret or anything.

I tell them a bit about Joe and all my fears about the Hot Italian Babe trying to steal him away from me, and how silly that is because Joe's great, but that it's hard to be more trusting when he hasn't said a word about her to me.

"You know how I am for conspiracy theories," Christina says when I've finished, which makes us laugh. "But I wouldn't trust that girl within fifty yards of *my* boyfriend."

"Dudette, don't break my heart like this." Zak falls on his knees at her feet and takes hold of her hands in a mock-pleading pose. "Tell me you don't have a boyfriend."

"Zak, I don't have a boyfriend," Christina tells him solemnly and pulls her hands away from him. Then, to me, she says, "You should fight dirtier."

"Fighting dirty isn't exactly . . . me," I tell her, although I appreciate that she's trying to be helpful.

"Well, Briddish, how's that working for you so far?"

I think of the pictures of Joe and HIB and then about how

he hasn't mentioned her to me. Hmm. She may have a point. "Not so good?"

Christina smiles, but it's not the nice kind. It's the kind of smile that says, "Exactly."

I think I could stand to get a little dirty.

Grandmother Gloria is going to be *so* thrilled!

Well, maybe not thrilled, it's hard to imagine her expressing a great deal of *any* kind of emotion, but maybe *satisfied* is the right word. I just hope it makes up for her disappointment last night, when Naomi and I both went with Jessica to get Will from the airport. I think Grandmother Gloria was looking forward to an evening of more booming Mozart and good manners, because she made a point of telling us that we didn't *all* need to go to get Will, and wouldn't it be nicer to stay home and improve ourselves?

Everyone else is already at the breakfast table, except for Will, Jessica, and Grandfather Rick. "Good morning, everyone," I say in a cheerful tone of voice, as I breeze into the room. "Did you all sleep well? I certainly did. Isn't it a lovely day?"

"Good morning," Naomi whispers, smiling her nervous smile, as she picks at her half slice of toast and half a grapefruit. That doesn't look like enough to keep a bird alive!

"Hmm?" Aunt Claire looks up from the paperwork she's reading through. "Oh, yes, it is a lovely day, isn't it? In more ways than one. I've got a very nice businessman who's interested in helping us raise funds for the homeless shelter."

"That's great, Aunt Claire, but don't you think you should take some time off? It's Saturday, after all."

"Er," she says, smiling vaguely as she ducks back into her paperwork.

"Good morning, Fiona," Grandmother Gloria's bland voice greets me, and she looks at her watch pointedly. Now that I know something about her past, and how she worries about everything, she doesn't seem anywhere near as intimidating as she did before. I'm really sorry I nicknamed her The Spider, too, even if it was only in my head.

"Sorry I'm a few minutes late," I jump in, because I know how particular Grandmother Gloria is about timekeeping.

"You're not the only one. William's still asleep, and Jessica went to the post office."

"Will was exhausted when we picked him up from the airport last night. He could do with some extra sleep," I say smoothly. "Anyway, there's a really good reason for my lateness. The deliveryman brought your new Ming replica, and I wanted to get it set up in the old one's place. You'd never know that corner of the hall was ever bare," I add.

I take my seat next to Aunt Claire, and Anne very kindly places my food in front of me. I also have half a grapefruit and half a slice of whole wheat toast on my plate.

"Oh." For once, Grandmother Gloria is speechless. Then she regains her composure. "Why, thank you, Fiona. There really was no need, but I do appreciate the gesture."

Is that an emotional gleam in her eye? I think so, but it's hard to tell.

"Mum's Sharon sorted it all out. Sharon is Mum's assistant. Mum says everybody needs a Sharon in their life."

We lapse into silence as everybody applies themselves to their respective grapefruits, too. It's not very filling, though, and I've finished it in about two minutes, even eating slowly. I think longingly of the pancakes and maple syrup I've gotten used to eating with Jessica in the kitchen.

I glance over at the sideboard, where there's a plate of toast and more grapefruit. There's also a selection of jams. I need at least quadruple what I've already had to fill my stomach. Breakfast is the most important meal of the day, after all.

Before I get up and help myself, though, I remember my manners. Rather, I anticipate what *Grandmother Gloria* considers manners. I think the steamroller effect I used the other day when Naomi and I wanted to swim would be a good one.

"Grandmother Gloria? I think I'd like some more toast. It's delicious and it would be a crime to let it go to waste, what with all the hunger in the world. And it's so important to be within one's Body Mass Index for health reasons, isn't it? Take me, for example. I'm five foot four and I weigh one hundred and fifteen pounds," I explain as I get to my feet. "No, it's okay, Anne, thank you. I'll help myself, because I want to choose some of those lovely-looking jams and I'm not sure what variety I want."

Anne, who is standing by the serving table with her arms folded across her ample bosom, gives me an encouraging smile. I smile back, but when Grandmother Gloria looks around to see who I'm smiling at, Anne's face falls blank.

"Anyway," I continue as Grandmother Gloria and Naomi watch me with amazement. Even Aunt Claire looks up from her paperwork. "My BMI is nineteen point seven, which is pretty low for someone of my height. According to the current medical opinion we should strive to achieve a BMI of between eighteen point five and twenty-five, which gives you quite a bit of range height-weight ratio-wise. Would you like some more toast, Naomi?"

"I—I. Sure. Yes, please."

"What kind of jam do you want? Why don't you come over and have a look?"

Naomi gets to her feet to join me. She pauses midstep when Grandmother Gloria finds her voice.

"Naomi, do you think that's wise, dear? You know how you struggle with your weight."

"I think Naomi has a lovely figure," I say and hold out the plate of toast to Naomi. She helps herself to some of it, and grins. "Personally, I think the Madrid fashion show organizers were right not to use models who have BMIs under eighteen," I push on. "Because models who are underweight are *bad* role models for young women. Teenage girls are susceptible to suggestion, and too-skinny models can promote things like anorexia. Or bulimia. Don't you agree, Grandmother?"

Grandmother Gloria looks across at me. "Oh. Well. Yes. It's very worrying."

"I mean, who ever heard of a size zero? How can anybody be a size zero? Wouldn't that make you nonexistent?"

"A lot of the people I deal with who are that size are homeless." Aunt Claire looks up from what she's doing. "Size zero isn't a fashion statement to them; it's a sad fact of life."

"That's terrible," I tell her. "But as people who are lucky to have enough to eat, we should take care not to develop eating disorders, shouldn't we?"

"I never looked at it that way before. I think I might have some more toast with jam. How about you, Mother?"

Come on, Grandmother Gloria, live dangerously for once, I think, as I take my place back at the table and bite into my toast. She could do with some of Anne's brownies, if you ask me. A pleasurable chocolate experience to make her even just a little bit happier.

"Not this time, thank you," she says, rather stuffily, and concentrates on sipping her coffee.

In between bites I make conversation to keep the gentle steamroller effect going. I tell them all about Daphne Kat, and Mum's studio, and who she knows and doesn't know. I mention her connection with Madonna.

"Your mother knows *Madonna*?" Naomi squeaks. "*The* Madonna? She's such a fashion icon," Naomi says, her eyes shining.

"Absolutely." I nod.

"A very charitable woman, I think," Aunt Claire says, and I'm doing a mental happy dance. This, I think, is the start of better mealtimes to come, even without Will.

Right at that moment, as I glance over at Naomi eating her toast, I get tingles at the back of my neck. *Oh, no.* What do they mean?

I pop the last bite of toast into my mouth as I try to figure out what's happening.

Then the tingles become strong prickles.

I wonder if this is the result of my ESP breakthrough at boot camp. Maybe it's a side effect of opening that window to my power. I don't think I'm in danger of getting overemotional, so I'm not afraid of an accidental ESP moment.

Then it happens.

It's as though my brain has been *hijacked* to a *parallel universe* again. Just like last Saturday on the Big Wheel.

Except this time the visions feature Grandmother Gloria instead of Naomi.

I see Grandmother Gloria following Anne around the house, criticizing her every move. I also see Grandmother Gloria on the telephone to her friends, moaning about Grandfather Rick. Grandmother Gloria, alone and unhappy in her gilded cage of a mansion. How sad is that?

Now I see Grandmother Gloria tweezing a hair from my hairbrush, because she's going to secretly arrange a DNA test to ensure that I really am Will's daughter. This would be *disastrous* on the secrecy-of-ESP front, because the last thing we need is for some clever non-espee geneticist to work out what the differences from average humans in our DNA sequences actually mean!

The image shifts and I see Will and myself being herded into a security van at *gunpoint*! Grandmother Gloria is standing on the veranda looking very miserable. All of Will's assets are seized, and the family is homeless!

Just when I am desperate to know what happens next and whether the Esper members will come to save us, the vision fades into an alternate vision of Grandmother Gloria. Grandfather Rick is spending a lot more time with her and she's smiling. They're going out to dinner together; they're playing golf together. Grandfather Rick joins in with family days by the pool, and Grandmother Gloria is relaxed and is even chilling with us—she's lying on a sunbed and eating a hamburger, even when Will isn't around to emit love vibes.

"Fiona, whatever is the matter with you?" Grandmother Gloria asks me, but I can hardly hear her because I'm overwhelmed. "Are you all right?"

If only she knew. "I'm fine, it's all fine," I say brightly. "May I please leave the table? I need to, um, do some, um, homework," I say, which is not the whole truth, but I do need to figure out what's going on.

As I reach my bedroom, another thought hits me. I wonder if I just experienced a deep level of precognition?

I think about telling Will what happened, but I dismiss that thought instantly. I can handle this myself. I mean, just because I had two strange precognitive moments about Naomi and Grandmother Gloria doesn't mean I need to go running to Will.

I decide that I am not going to worry. While I wait for Will to wake up and see what we're doing today, I am going to practice controlling my power (just in case). Which I will do right after I e-mail Joe.

Now, how to fight dirty, like Christina suggested?

I have a flash of inspiration. This morning the e-mail I had from him included a detailed diagram of the dirt layers and iridium found at the K-T boundary. I send him the following e-mail:

To: "Joe Summers" <OccamsRazor@sciencenet.com>

From: "Fiona Blount" <MarieCurieGirl@bluesky.com>

Subject: Re: K-T Boundary

Interesting diagram. I love it when you talk dirt to me!

(See attached pic.)

The picture I sent is one I took myself of my lips kissing the camera lens.

I think that makes my point.

Now for some shield and focus practice, I think, feeling pleased with myself. In fact, so pleased with myself that I am going to actually draw in power. I know it's against the rules, but how will I ever be able to help my family if I don't break a few small rules?

1. Close eyes.
2. Picture room in mind containing magnet and slightly ajar window.
3. Picture gravitons flooding into magnet, and Peaceflower's crystal just outside window, a pinpoint of light in the dark.
4. Picture very small amount of evaporation/will escaping into crystal.
5. Hold it in crystal.
6. Build shield.
7. Focus beam of light contained within crystal onto shield.
8. Release will.

Instead of applying my will to just my shield, I wonder if I could try applying it to something else, simultaneously? Like the pencil on my desk. I think about it moving from one side of the desk to the other. I can see the pencil rolling across the desk in my mind. I follow all the appropriate steps and . . .

"Fiona, are you in there? Can I come in?" It's Will. I feel instantly guilty because I'm not supposed to be doing any ESP practice away from Esper Hall. Well, apart from visualizing my shield and holding it in my mind at all times.

"Of course," I call back, release my power into the universe, and put down Peaceflower's crystal.

"Am I interrupting anything important?" Will smiles as he comes into the room. "No urgent instant messages or e-mails from Italy?"

"Absolutely not," I say, leaning over from my chair to pat the bed. "Take a pew."

"I wanted to check our plans for today," he says. He looks so tired, despite his smile. He's flying back to L.A. on Monday, and I think he only came home at all because of me.

"How about a down day?" I suggest. "We could, you know, just hang by the pool, barbecue, and not do anything much. Then we could go into Manhattan tomorrow."

"Are you sure it's what *you* want to do? You're not suggesting Manhattan to make other people happy?"

"Of course not." In that moment I nearly tell him about my precognitive moment with Naomi and my concerns about the family, but I don't. I need to be a rock of support for him, not a burden.

"I thought you wanted to go to the Liberty Science Center."

"I do, and we will, but I thought that Naomi might not be that interested. See, it's the perfect way for you and me to spend father/daughter time together. Jessica's into all of the fashiony stuff, just like Naomi. We could, oh, do touristy stuff, while they go to the boutiques. Then we could all meet up for lunch. What do you think?"

"Father/daughter time sounds great," he says, reaching across and hugging me. "You've been here for more than a week and I've barely seen you."

"At least we get to chat on the phone every day," I reassure him, then we both laugh as his stomach growls.

"I need breakfast," he admits, getting to his feet and kissing me on the head. "Great news on the you-know-what breakthrough, too."

"I had help," I say modestly, but I am feeling pleased with myself.

Once Will leaves, I start the process with the shield and pencil all over again. I focus; I concentrate on the pencil on my desk. ROLL, PENCIL. ROLL.

So of course there's another knock at my door.

I release my will. The pencil snaps in two, and I jump. Oops. It's not exactly what I intended, but I did manage to do something to it with my ESP. Sighing, I cross to the door.

"I—I wanted to say thank you for what you did at breakfast." It's Naomi. "With the weight thing. I thought Grandmother Gloria was going to self-implode from shock when you said that about Madrid's fashion week."

"I used to be more keep-my-mouth-shut-and-stay-low," I say to Naomi. "But sometimes we have to stick up for ourselves. We don't have to be rude or loud about it, but when something is important to us, I think we have a right to speak up. Like your mum does for disadvantaged people." I say the last part because I want to encourage Naomi, and it *is* true. "Aunt Claire *isn't* afraid to speak her mind."

"Yeah, she speaks her mind all right, as long as it's to help strangers."

"She's very vocal about good causes. I admire that."

"Yeah." Naomi pauses. "Mom hasn't always been like that. All sad and throwing herself into charity work. She used to be really bubbly and happy, but then after the divorce she just seemed to lose herself. She lost Dad and got stuck with me."

"Hey, it's not your fault." I look at Naomi earnestly. "Grown-ups fall in and out of love, have their own problems—we shouldn't take it personally. I didn't take it personally when Mum accidentally lost Dad at the Glastonbury Music Festival. If I had, I wouldn't be here now."

"I'm glad you're here."

"You are? You're not, you know, upset that I'm the new illegitimate girl on the block, here to drag the family's name through the mud and steal Will's fortune away from the rest of the family?" I say this in a theatrical tone of voice, but with undertones of Grandmother Gloria.

"No." Naomi laughs. "I think you've made things a lot more interesting. Um, if you don't mind me asking, what is that picture on your laptop?"

It's a diagram of the K-T dirt layer. My new wallpaper. "It's a photo my boyfriend sent to remind me of him while I'm away," I tell her happily.

"I've never had a boyfriend," she confides. "It doesn't help if you go to an all-girl private school like me."

"No." I laugh.

"I don't get out too often, which doesn't help, either. Grandmother Gloria and Mom worry that something will happen to me."

I roll my eyes. Then, I ask her, "What would you do if you could get a bit more freedom?"

"Oh, I don't know. Go into Manhattan by myself, visit museums, window-shop in the Village—" She pauses, and glances down at her pleated skirt and frilly blouse. "Yeah, it's hard to believe that I love designing clothes."

"I think you look very nice." It's true, her clothes are very nice. But—

"But out-of-date?"

"Well—"

"It's okay, Fiona, you won't hurt my feelings. It's easier to let someone else make the decisions about what I wear. You can probably imagine what shopping with Grandmother is like. But I wish I could have the kind of clothes you wear."

"Me?" I glance down at my khakis and pink T with the words BITE ME across the front. "I'm hardly the queen of fashion. They're just practical and comfortable in the summer heat. Actually, my mum was the one who chose them."

"Well, it was a good choice of T-shirt for breakfast this morning," she says, and we both laugh.

There's a brief silence as she glances around my room.

"Don't you have your own TV?"

"No," I tell her.

"But what do you do with no TV? Especially in the evenings." She sounds completely shocked, and her eyes are as wide as saucers.

"Oh, go online, read, that kind of thing. To be honest, this last week I've been so tired by jet lag, and the hard work at science camp, it hasn't really been an issue."

"Would—would you like to come and watch TV with me? *The Apartment* is on."

The Apartment is always on, I think, and watching Dude is so not what I want to do; I want to practice my focus and release skills, but this is important to Naomi. In fact, I could practice gathering and releasing my will while pretending to watch Dude. I slip Peaceflower's crystal into my pocket.

"I'd love to," I tell her. Also, I'm curious to see inside her bedroom, because bedrooms say a lot about a person, don't they?

Her bedroom walls are cream-colored, offset by the white door and window frames, a pretty neutral backdrop upon which an artist (which Naomi clearly is) can stamp her identity. Naomi's particular stamp is a combination of natural fibers, faux animal skins, and bright jags of modern art on her walls.

"This is amazing," I tell her as I walk over to her desk, where she has a corkboard pinned behind her computer. It's covered in designs for cute pants and tops, all for girls of a normal, healthy size. It's very teen culture, but with an intriguing fusion of lace trims and animal patterns.

"These are really good. Really good. Did you draw them?"

"Um, yes." She blushes. "I'd love to design my own line of clothes."

"Is that what you're going to do after high school?"

"Oh, no, that would be frivolous, according to Grandmother Gloria and Mom. They say I need skills that will prepare me for a job, and earn me a good salary, because we can't all depend on Uncle Will forever." She touches a design—washed-out jeans with intricately embroidered star signs, and a figure-hugging top in pale green with matching embroidery—and sighs.

"Once upon a time, Mom might have thought design school was a good idea, but her experience with the divorce really shook her foundations. She's into safety, these days."

"What did your mom do before?"

Naomi walks across the room toward the TV. "Dad's an attorney and earns good money, so she didn't have to work. I guess she was a professional wife and mother. You know, involved with the PTA, lunching with her friends, shopping, throwing parties for Dad's work colleagues. When he moved out, she didn't have anything left. Except me." Naomi laughs drily. "What a bargain." Before I can say anything to try to make her feel better, she turns to me. "Ready for *The Apartment*?"

"Yes, great!" I feign enthusiasm.

After fifteen minutes of Dude cavorting in the pool with the skeletal female members of *The Apartment* (it's quite luxurious compared to the U.K. version), playing loud music in the living room while dancing around like he's a pop hero, and discussing his plans for his book, *My Life So Far*, with the camera (and the millions of disenfranchised youths he apparently resonates with), I'm bored. I glance sideways at Naomi. She's hanging on his every word. She won't notice if I close my eyes and practice gathering and releasing my will. Practice makes perfect.

I push my hand into my pocket and hold Peaceflower's crystal in my palm. Madeline says that I shouldn't really need a physical embodiment of my imagination, and that I'll probably grow past it. But for now it's comforting.

I gather gravitons, and focus a teeny stream of them through the window in my mind and into the crystal. I focus on the crystal, but an image of the TV pops into my mind as I hear Dude's voice. Why am I thinking of the TV? I don't want to do anything to it. I wipe the TV image and replace it with the vast emptiness of the universe and harmlessly disperse my will into it. I do this about ten times, then, I think, why not gather just a little bit more of my will to expand my ability? Just a teeny bit more . . . Yes, I did it!

"Zoe is, like, a megabaybe," I hear Dude say.

"Oh, no," Naomi says as I am about to try it again.

I open my eyes. Dude appears to be whispering to the camera in the bathroom. I gather in and focus more of my will as I phase him out.

"She's so totally hot," he adds quietly. "But then I only go for totally hot babes. She's waiting for me right now in her bedroom."

"This is awful," Naomi moans as I contain my will in my crystal in the background while I focus on the TV. "He's adorable, but doesn't he see that he's worth more than all the Zoes and Barbies who throw themselves at him? I really wish he'd grow up and be a man instead of a silly boy who thinks scoring girls is cool." Naomi touches my arm just as I am about to release my will, and I think, *I agree with you.*

I open my eyes and release my will at *Dude Mann on TV*, instead of dispersing it to the universe as a whole. The TV goes fuzzy, just for a few seconds, and just as I am thinking, *Oh, no, I've broken the TV*, the picture comes back.

Whew. No harm done.

Okay. I've been thinking about it all day, while we were swimming and barbecuing. I didn't have any more of those precognitive moments, and if they were that meaningful, you'd think that I'd have them more than *once* about each person, wouldn't you? So I shouldn't jump to any conclusions. I'm going to think it through for a while.

In the meantime, I have had a small success with pencil rolling. I gather my will and log on to e-mail at the same time.

To: "Fiona Blount" <MarieCurieGirl@bluesky.com>

From: "Joe Summers" <OccamsRazor@sciencenet.com>

Subject: Fish!

MCG, love the lips. I saw the attached picture and thought of you.

The title of his e-mail doesn't sound romantic, but when I open the attachment I see a pair of gorgeous yellow angelfish kissing!

Take that, HIB, I think. I shield, focus, and release my will on a nonbroken pencil. It rolls slowly across my desk.

"Fiona, are you still awake?" Naomi asks as she knocks on my door.

"Come in," I say as I close down Joe's e-mail.

"You're never going to believe this," she tells me breathlessly as she closes the door and walks over to me. "It's Dude. He's turning over a new leaf."

"What?"

"He said it just now, on national TV. He thinks it's time he grew up and took responsibility for his actions. Isn't it spooky that I said that near-same thing this morning when we were watching him?"

"Very spooky," I tell her as the enormity of what might have happened hits me. "Maybe he just saw the error of his ways?"

Or maybe he had unexpected help.

Tra-la-la, compelling people to do things is *such* a lot of *fun.* I am still feeling secretly smug about the possibility that I changed Dude for the better.

I quash the teeny, nagging, guilty voice in my brain saying it's wrong to mess with other people's minds. I mean, Dude is such a reformed person, he's an asset to the human race.

Compulsion, yay, I think, as Jessica and I drive to Esper Hall.

Oh. That's my cell phone ringing. It's Mum. We've been playing phone tag over the weekend, and it's Tuesday already. I feel a bit guilty for not having e-mailed her, but life has been busy.

"Hi, Fabulous Fiona." Then she lowers her voice to a whisper. "How are things going with your grandmother? Did the Ming Thing get resolved?"

"It's okay, we can talk normally. I'm in the car with Jessica." Hearing her name, Jessica smiles at me. "The Ming arrived Saturday, and Grandmother Gloria nearly teared up. At least I thought she did."

"She mentioned it to me on Sunday," Jessica says. "She seemed happy about it. That is, as far as she can seem happy about anything. Personally, I think it's ugly. No offense."

"Good," Mum tells me at the same time. "Personally, I thought it was ugly, but there's no accounting for taste."

"That's exactly what Jessica just said."

"So how about everything else? You getting on well with Naomi?" Mum asks.

"You were right—it was just a case of taking the time to get to know her a bit. We've been swimming nearly every day, and I've been watching the American version of *The Flat* with her."

"We all know how much you love Dude Mann," Mum says as Jessica rolls her eyes. "So, I've got a cup of coffee, I'm sitting comfortably, tell me everything you've been up to. If you've got time."

I tell her all about Saturday, and how we made a real family day of it. Burgers, sausages, spareribs, yum. And that Grandmother Gloria was out at one of her ladies' club things, but we managed to persuade Grandfather Rick to leave the confines of his basement to come up for some food. He only stayed for a few minutes—he had an idea for a design to keep the bugs away from the water. It was nice to see him, but there is no way to keep him out of the basement when he has one of his ideas. Even Aunt Claire came out to eat barbecue with us, which made Naomi really happy.

Then when Mum prods me about Sunday and Manhattan, I tell her all about breakfast at the Carnegie Deli, famous for its pastrami and the rudeness of its waiters. It was a good thing Jessica had warned us about the size of the sandwiches—even though we only ordered two sandwiches between four of us, it was still a lot.

"Then Jessica and Naomi went downtown to check out the latest fashions at some of the shops in SoHo and NoLIta, which apparently stands for North of Little Italy, while Will and I played tourist. We walked around Central Park for a while, then we got a bicycle rickshaw down Fifth Avenue to the Empire State Building. That was a pretty death-defying experience in Manhattan traffic."

"Sounds like you're having a blast," Mum says, and I can hear the smile in her voice. "What else did you do?"

"Grand Central Terminal, because I wanted to see the constellations in the ceiling, then we met Jessica and Naomi in Times Square. After lunch we took the bus downtown and got the ferry to the Statue of Liberty, then Ellis Island. Oh, I forgot, while we were on Fifth Avenue Will took me into an electronics store and bought me a webcam. You must get Sharon to install one on your computer—then we'd be able to see each other as well as hear each other," I tell her.

"Aw, you know me and computers, Fiona."

"This, from the woman who uses state-of-the-art electronics for her craft." We both laugh at that. "Anyway, we picked up pizza on the way home. Grandmother Gloria was all pizza this, and fast food that, but Will persuaded her to try a bite. I think she only did it to please him, because you could see the look of horror on her face as she imagined the calories sliding down her throat. Then the gorgeousness of it hit her taste buds and she tried a bit more."

"Sounds like a positive breakthrough."

"Yeah." I smile. Then I realize that she's let me blather on and on about what I've been doing, but not said a word about herself. "So what's new with you and Mark and Daphne Kat?"

"Oh, same old, same old," she says lightly, but I sense that something is wrong.

I don't push it because Mum might not like me asking personal questions in front of Jessica, but I resolve to call her later as we say good-bye.

"Everything all right?" Jessica asks as we approach the Esper Hall shield.

"Nothing that can't be fixed," I tell her.

Because even if they've had a tiff or something, Mum and Mark clearly love each other, and I could always help them out with a bit of you-know-what. Once they're talking it over, it shouldn't be too difficult to fix things for them. I mean, it would be totally wrong to compel people to fall in love, but if they already love each other anyway, then a bit of help isn't really wrong, is it?

Tra-la-la. I am such a compulsion queen.

I am still a compulsion queen!

This afternoon Christina and I have been working as a team to practice our compulsion on each other. We've been catching up with everybody else for the last couple of days, but I can now safely say that we're caught up. It's going *really* well.

I gather my will, focus it on her, and release it. Christina jumps up and down, then pirouettes around the room.

After a minute, when she doesn't stop, Mr. Rafaelle, our compulsion teacher for today, tells Jack and Serena, our empath minders, to step in. "Nice, Fiona, but try to use a little less force," he tells me. "Actually, a lot less."

Okay. Less force next time.

"Nice one, Briddish," Christina tells me, gasping. "I am so getting you back for that."

It's a very weird experience being compelled by Christina. I don't even know it's happening to me; it seems entirely normal to climb onto my chair and sing Lily Allen's "Smile" at the top of my lungs, shaking my booty as I do it. Thankfully, it wears off after about thirty seconds.

"I have to say it, dudette, even though your mom is some kind of pop star, I wouldn't plan on following in her footsteps anytime soon." Zak's been holding his hands over his ears. I know. I can't sing to save my life.

"Blame Christina." I grin. She's holding her hands over her ears, too.

"Is it safe yet?" Christina also has her eyes squeezed shut.

"I don't think you sounded that bad," April says, although I did see her grimacing a moment ago.

"Okay, your turn for torture." I point to Christina with a smirk.

I close my eyes, take a deep breath, gather my will, and focus it on her again.

Christina places a hand on her hip, bats her eyelashes at us, and flounces around the room.

"My name is Christina, and my one wish for humankind is for world peace," she says in a singsong voice. We all fall over laughing, bccause today's outfit (which is in her normal vein of black with skulls and crossbones) is not conducive to any kind of beauty pageant.

But when she doesn't stop after about a minute, Mr. Rafaelle and our empaths have to step in again. Okay. I definitely need to tone it down.

"That is such a totally weird feeling," Christina says in her normal voice once she's been restored. "I can't believe I just did those things. But I forgive you, Briddish."

"I thought that was great." Zak whistles. "You can be my Miss New Jersey anytime. Can we be partners, next time? I *so* want to try my skills on you."

"Are you kidding me? You'd probably make me do something inappropriate and against my nature. Like kiss you."

"Okay, class," Mr. Rafaelle tells us as the bell rings. "Lunchtime. But a word of caution—you've picked up this skill amazingly quickly. I can't remember when a class has achieved so much in such a short time. Remember not to get too bigheaded. You're still novices."

We traipse off to the Esper cafeteria.

I know what the Esper rules say about not affecting someone's mind, but let's face it: All I want to do is help my family in a small way. Where's the harm in that? It's no worse than the things that us students do to one another all of the time here at boot camp. Although we do have Jack and Serena around in case anything goes wrong. . . .

I am dying to tell someone about my success with Dude. However, a little voice at the back of my mind is worrying about using excessive force after Mr. Rafaelle's warning. As we line up and get our food (burgers today), I wonder how I can approach this without giving myself away.

Christina leads the way to an empty table, but there are other groups of students and Esper employees seated all around, and I don't want to risk the chance of being overheard.

"How about the table over there?" I say, indicating one in an unpopulated corner of the room.

"Whatever," Christina says with a shrug. "A table's a table."

"So, what do we, um, think about using ESP for the greater good?" I casually ask April and Christina once we're settled.

"I think we shouldn't do it, because it says so in the rules." April bites into her burger. "After all, the rules are there to *protect* us."

"Why do you ask?" Christina asks in a suspicious tone of voice.

"I was just making polite conversation." I shrug, and Christina raises her eyebrows at me. "But just say, theoretically, that I—no, not I as in me, personally—somebody with ESP used it on a person who was appearing on a live-stream TV show. Do you think it would work?"

"Ah, you mean as a TV science experiment, quantum thing?"

"Yes, exactly that. A science experiment." Whew. Excellent suggestion by April.

"Well," Christina begins. "If ESP theory is tied so closely with quantum theory, and they're sure shoving it down our throats here, then it's not beyond the realm of possibility that it works that way with ESP and TV, too."

"All those parallel universes and disappearing and reappearing particles. Why should this sound any crazier than that?" April asks. Then she shakes her head. "I still don't *get* it."

Christina puts down her veggie burger and looks me in the eye. "*Briddish.* I'd never have pegged you as a rule breaker." She stares at me for a few seconds more, then throws back her head and laughs. "My God, they say it's always the quiet ones."

"What?" I ask innocently and dip a fry into my ketchup, but I know I'm blushing. "I was just, you know, asking. Opening a topic of conversation."

"What's the topic?" Zak's voice comes from behind me and I jump.

"I wondered how long it would take you to show up," Christina tells him.

"Dudette, there's only one cafeteria and we all gotta eat," he says, pulling up his chair to the table.

"Yeah, one cafeteria and all those *empty* tables surrounding us. Well, this is delightful," Christina says sarcastically, but with a hint of laughter in her tone so we know she's joking. "My own personal lapdog, after only a week and a half. That's so sweet, so tender."

"We were just talking about ESP and quantum particle experiments on live TV," April fills him in. "Fiona was wondering if you could compel somebody on live TV without being present in the same location."

"I can see the logic of that, dudes." Zak tries to swipe a sip of Christina's soda, but she slaps him on the hand. "What?"

"I want the particles of this particular soda in *my* stomach," she snipes at him, in an affectionate kind of way.

"Dudette, you're a hard woman," Zak tells her.

"Getting back on topic, is everybody shielded?" Christina asks. We all nod, then she looks at me. "Briddish here was about to tell us how she's been abusing the rules and using ESP outside of boot camp. What, exactly, did you do to Dude Mann?"

My God. She guessed. I should never underestimate Christina.

"No way." Zak laughs.

I sigh. There's no point keeping it to myself. I tell them what happened, including the spooky alternate-universe visions I've had for Naomi, and how much she loves Dude, and how it would have really made her flip if Dude had made out with that other woman on *The Apartment.*

"But the point is, I didn't mean to do it," I add.

Zak and April are looking at me with their mouths wide-open. Christina, however, nods with approval. "You know what I think? That rules are meant to be broken. Who is Esper to tell us what we can or can't do with our powers?" And then, "Ha ha ha, I can't believe you accidentally compelled Dude, Briddish. I bet you couldn't do it on purpose."

"I could," I say, indignant. "When I've had a bit more practice."

"But it's wrong." April is clearly shocked.

"Well, I guess we should go and check out what Dude's up to, just to verify this." Zak gets to his feet.

"Where are you going?"

"To watch *The Apartment* in the Esper Hall TV room."

Five minutes later we're glued to the TV.

Dude Mann is vacuuming the apartment and planning what he's going to cook for the other inhabitants from their supplies tonight.

"It will be megadelicious," he tells the camera. "An yer know what? It feels so good to be a contributing, useful member of society."

I know how that feels.

The bell rings. Time for class. As we leave the TV room, Christina takes my arm to hold me back.

"You should think about accidentally fixing the Hot Italian Babe," she tells me.

"I can't fix her if I don't know what she's done, though. I mean, as far as I know she's just in the photos and with Joe at her dad's lab. Those are hardly crimes, are they?"

"Your choice, your loss. Maybe you should use your powers on your cousin—she sounds screwed up," she adds. "I dare you to fix her life, like you fixed Dude's."

As if I could be lured into a dare! Although, Dude is truly improved. And *I* did it. And I'm pretty sure that, though it was an accident, I could do it again.

Superherodom, here I come.

Chapter 13

"You know, it's just a minor thing but please humor me. Why are you wearing sunglasses in your bedroom?" Will laughs at me via Skype (which has been secured with some Esper technology, of course).

"Well, as the daughter of a superhero I felt it only right to follow the family tradition." I laugh along with him and take them off. "I may have to start wearing tights and a cape, too."

"Could this have to do with a breakthrough today, I wonder?" Will holds his chin and tilts his head. "Jess mentioned earlier when I spoke to her that you'd had more success at boot camp, but she didn't tell me *what.* So come on. What happened?"

"Well, this morning she let me use her as an ESP target so that I could practice on someone with really strong powers. I couldn't break through her shield at first, but when she let it down a little I managed to get through. I compelled her to do the cancan dance around the classroom and hum the music at the same time."

"Ha ha ha. I can guess she was *thrilled* about that."

"She was a good sport about it. She was really good, actually. She can kick her legs really high. Anyway, she got me back by compelling me to do push-ups, even though I had my shield up. She's really strong."

I mean, why push-ups? Jessica told me it was because physical exertion helps you focus your mind more. I got this very strange feeling in my brain while I was doing them. A feeling of cognitive dissonance, and my mind was trying to fight back against the compulsion. Jessica said that it was because as our skills are developing we're becoming aware of others using their powers on us. We have to learn to resist compulsion.

"I'm really proud of you. You're doing so well after only a week and a half, Fiona," Will tells me with a smile, and I glow with pleasure.

"Um, how's the other business? You know. With your new espee."

"She called today, but she's still too scared to reveal her identity." Will isn't smiling anymore. "I told her she didn't need to do that, she could use a fake name for now. I'm really worried because she asked questions about compulsion. Like, what would happen if she accidentally compelled her sister to jump off a bridge in the middle of an argument," he continues in a very worried tone of voice.

"Oh. That's not good. She didn't actually *do* that, did she?"

"No. She stopped herself in time. But what if she can't do that *next* time? And you realize what this means, don't you?"

"You have a possible second espee in her sister," I say as the light dawns in my brain.

"Exactly. Which would make three, counting her famous parent, who would also have to be an espee." Will shakes his head. "We've managed to get our hands on more of the old clinical records, which show more names we didn't have, but no famous names."

"What if the famous person changed his or her name officially?" I ask him. "Because people in the music industry do it all the time. Sir Elton John, for example. His original name was Reginald Kenneth Dwight, which doesn't have the same kind of star-quality ring, does it? And, of course, there's Dude Mann."

"Fiona, you're a genius," he tells me, and I feel even more warm and fuzzy. "Why didn't *we* think of that?"

"Aw, I have my uses," I say with a grin.

"Okay, sweetie. I want to get started on this right away. How about we chat tomorrow evening, same time?"

"That would be great," I tell him. "And the next day's Friday, so we'll be able to chat in person. Naomi and I will come with Jessica to collect you."

"Can't wait," he says before disconnecting.

I hope Grandmother Gloria isn't too disappointed that Naomi and I will miss another Friday night of self-improvement, I think, as I log on to e-mail. Yay. E-mails from Joe and Gina. I open Gina's first.

To: "Fiona Blount" <MarieCurieGirl@bluesky.com>
From: "Gina Duffy" <Feminista@bluesky.com>
Subject: Homeward Bound

Sorry—meant to e-mail you yesterday but we all went to the beach to get away from the heat in the city. It was fun, I suppose, but I WISH we were all home instead. I miss Kieran.

Anyway, the place was called Ostia Lido and it had black sand. I've attached some pix.

She wishes they were all home? I thought they were having a lot of fun in Rome. I open Gina's pictures. It *looks* like they had a lot of fun. Especially Isabella and Joe. In every single shot the HIB is practically draped around Joe's neck. Is Gina trying to tell me something without actually saying it?

My earlier self-satisfaction dissolves, and I remember what Christina said about fixing the HIB. . . .

I should be more sure of myself, but the HIB is stunning in a yellow-and-black bikini. How could anyone resist her? How could Joe resist her? I open Joe's e-mail.

To: "Fiona Blount" <MarieCurieGirl@bluesky.com>
From: "Joe Summers" <OccamsRazor@sciencenet.com>
Subject: Black Sand

Mucho lazing on beach with friends and Family Fiori, mucho eating, mucho fun. My luggage doesn't know what it's missing. Pix attached.

xx OR

I open the photos. They feature Joe posing like a calendar model on the beach, dipping his toes in the sea, and trying on Gina's and Peaceflower's silly 1950s sunglasses, as though he doesn't have a care in the world. How can he mention the Fiori family and not mention the fact that he's on the beach with their gorgeous daughter?

I can't go on like this! I have to ask him about the HIB.

I glance back through Gina's photos and type a reply to Joe.

To: "Joe Summers" <OccamsRazor@sciencenet.com>

From: "Fiona Blount" <MarieCurieGirl@bluesky.com>

Subject: Hot Italian Babe

I can see that you're having a fabulous time. Gina's photo showed me just how totally fabulous.

I attach one of Gina's Joe/HIB photos and hit "send" before I can change my mind.

As I knock on Naomi's bedroom door to see if she's ready for our regular evening swim, I'm worried that I've made a huge mistake. I need to work off some of my stress and induce some endorphins, so the exercise will do me extra good tonight.

"Dude's on *Dr. Phil*," Naomi tells me breathlessly when she opens the door. "I can't miss this. Can we swim later?"

"Sure thing," I tell her, thinking that maybe watching the effect of my superhero powers will distract me from worries about Joe.

I know I shouldn't be smug, but I can't help but think that Dude really *does* seem to have changed for the better.

"It was incredible, Dr. Phil. It was one of those—wot do you call them?—oh, yeah—epifyny fing moments. Road to Damascus stuff," he explains via a video link from *The Apartment.*

"Dude isn't supposed to leave the apartment at all while he's still a contender," Naomi says, her eyes glued to the screen. "But he's the hottest news item at the moment, so the show came to him. Can you believe it? The stars come to *him.* I really liked Dude before, but the new him is *so* much better," she tells me happily.

"Absolutely," I agree with Naomi, trying not to let my secret success go to my head.

"I realized that my life was a meaningless vacuum of fun and partying," Dude tells the camera, a soulful expression on his face. "You gotta have meaning, you gotta have love for your fellow men, I mean 'people,'" he says, making speech marks with his fingers. "You've got to be sensitive to other people and use the right language—Zoe keeps reminding me about that. But wivout meaning and love, why bovver?"

"So true." Naomi turns to me. "Just like my love for Dude gives meaning to *my* life. It's like he can read my *mind.*"

If only Naomi knew that some people really can read minds. I can't wait to develop that particular skill. It would certainly be helpful for figuring out why my boyfriend is secretive about his beautiful new friend. Is he just trying to

be nice until he can break up with me in person?

"Anyway, Zoe, where are you, luv?" Dude goes off camera for a moment and reappears with the gorgeous, very skinny brunette he was planning on snogging last Saturday when I accidentally compelled him.

I get a really bad feeling in my stomach and instant prickles at the back of my neck.

"Me and Zoe, we got an announcement to make. We've decided to make our love official and get engayged."

"What?" Naomi yells at the TV. "He's only known her for a little over a week. How can it be true love so quickly?"

I hold my breath as I glance sideways at Naomi. Her face falls and she clutches my arm. I can see actual tears in her eyes!

Dr. Phil is congratulating them. All of *The Apartment* contenders are hugging them. Then Dude kisses Zoe very passionately, and Naomi squeezes my arm even harder. She moans, like a hurt animal.

"I think I need chocolate," she tells me and pulls a plastic container—a secret stash of food—out from under her bed. "I need lots of chocolate—do you want some, Fiona?"

As I stare at the chocolate bars in the container, I get the same precognitive flash I had about Naomi the other day. Oh, no! My worst fears for her are coming true. But, I have to ask myself, did I cause the actual problem in the first place by accidentally compelling Dude to be good, or would Naomi have become equally upset if Dude had had lots of different girlfriends, rather than one fiancée?

The vision in my mind grows stronger as Naomi eats first one chocolate bar, then another. Christina's right. I have to *do* something.

I open the window in my mind, clutch the crystal in my pocket, and gather my will.

"There's more to life than Dude," I tell her gently. "Look at everything you've got going for you. You've got a great figure, great bone structure—a lot of people would kill for that, by the way—and additionally you're a fabulous clothing designer. I bet a lot of guys would want to date you, if only they met you—you need to let yourself live a little."

"It's sweet of you to try to cheer me up," she says between bites, wiping her eyes with her tissue. "But I'm not like you. I wish I could be!"

Naomi blows her nose and opens another chocolate bar. I *can't* let her ruin her life!

Should I or shouldn't I? I mean, affecting Dude was accidental, but it's been a complete success. I decide I am going to help Naomi. It's the superhero thing to do, after all.

"Naomi, look at me," I say to her, my decision made.

I gather my will and focus. FEEL GOOD ABOUT YOURSELF, NAOMI, I think. DON'T LOVE DUDE ANYMORE. YOU ARE A GREAT DESIGNER; FOCUS ON THAT. YOU ARE ALSO A PRETTY GIRL, AND THERE ARE MORE POTENTIAL BOYFRIENDS FOR YOU. THINK ABOUT WHAT YOU WANT OUT OF LIFE AND DO IT.

Then I release my will on her.

Her eyes widen for a moment, and then she says, "Do you know what? I'm feeling better. You have a way of cheering people up. You're right," she adds, putting the chocolate bar away. "I should make the most of myself, and I'm going to start right now."

This is excellent. If I can't be happy myself, I can at least make others happy, instead.

Naomi switches off the TV. "Want to go for a swim?"

Absolutely.

To: "Fiona Blount" <MarieCurieGirl@bluesky.com>
From: "Joe Summers" <OccamsRazor@sciencenet.com>
Subject: Re: Hot Italian Babe

What? Are you jealous? You don't trust me?

To: "Joe Summers" <OccamsRazor@sciencenet.com>
From: "Fiona Blount" <MarieCurieGirl@bluesky.com>
Subject: Re: Re: Hot Italian Babe

I didn't say I don't trust you. I'm just wondering why you hadn't mentioned her, since you're obviously very close.

To: "Fiona Blount" <MarieCurieGirl@bluesky.com>
From: "Joe Summers" <OccamsRazor@sciencenet.com>
Subject: Re: Re: Re: Hot Italian Babe

Which means you don't trust me.

I think we've just had our first fight. Or is it the end of our relationship?

I burst into tears and bury my head in my pillow.

"Way to go, dudette," Zak congratulates me the next day when we are practicing telekinesis. I have just lifted the small trash can and moved it from one end of the room to the other. Okay, so I crashed it a bit when I released it to the floor, but overall that was pretty good, I think, trying hard to keep my thoughts off Joe.

"Oh, I can tell you're going to be just as strong as dear William." Miss Bird claps her tiny hands together with delight. "But remember what you've been studying in theory. You have to draw less force, think of the gravitons sliding gently out of the different dimensions to the magnet, remember that wisp of steam flowing out of the window of your mind."

"Hey, you're supposed to be *my* adoring hero." Christina nudges Zak in the ribs and places her hand on her hip. "My turn." She frowns in concentration, releases her will onto the trash can, and it flies across the room, nearly hitting Mehreen and Farah, who duck just in time.

"Dear, I said *less* force, not more," Miss Bird tuts. "Gently does it."

"Yeah, whatever," Christina says, flashing me a "See? I can do it, too" look. I grin at her. We've been competing to see who is stronger, her or me, but in a friendly way. It's a good distraction from boyfriend problems. So far we're pretty equal.

"Way to go to you, too, dudette. My turn." Zak concentrates. He lifts the trash can a few feet in the air, but then it comes crashing back to the floor. "I guess I need more practice."

"Or maybe you have to accept that us girls are stronger than you. I always thought girls had better mental control," Christina teases him.

"Now, now, it's not a competition," Miss Bird warns us. "Some of us are better at other things." She's right. Zak's really good at shielding. That's what we've moved on to in compulsion periods—trying to compel one another even when we have our shields raised.

"Christina likes him, really," April whispers to me, then she turns to the trash can. Majestically, it rises from the ground, moves steadily through the air, and settles on the opposite side of the room with barely a scraping of its metal bottom.

"Excellent progress," Miss Bird praises her as the bell for lunch rings.

"That proves my point," Christina tells Zak when we troop to the cafeteria.

"Hey, I'm comfortable with my limits." How sweet is that? Some boys can't handle a girl being better. Then again, he's in love with Christina, and she's hardly a pushover with or without her strong ESP skills.

Once we've all gotten our food and sit ourselves down at a remote table, Christina nods to Zak.

"Okay, Shield Guy, do your stuff."

During class, we've been very careful not to talk about Dude and the change in him. We were even trying not to think about him. As Christina said, the walls have ears and eyes around here, and if someone forgets to shield I'm done.

Everyone agrees. All for one, and one for all, just like the Three Musketeers and D'Artagnan. Except we are the Three Esperteers and Z'Aktagnan. It's really sweet of them to want to protect me.

Z'Aktagnan's strong shielding is very useful, too, because he can extend his far enough to cover all of us even when we're shielding ourselves. It's a double blanket of security.

"About your meddling, Briddish," Christina says as soon as Zak gives her the thumbs-up on the shield. "I've got to say it, but way to go. That Dude guy is much better behaved." Praise indeed from Christina. "Better to the point of boring and there *isn't* any point watching *The Apartment* anymore," she adds with a wry smile. "I guess that's the flip side of using our powers."

"But a good flip side, yes?" I look anxiously from April to Christina to Zak.

"Oh, you didn't! You didn't use your powers on someone else, did you?" April asks me. Then slumps back in her seat. "Oh. You did. I think I'd be too scared, in case it went wrong."

"It hasn't gone wrong," I say, thinking of the positive results so far.

"I'm beginning to like your style, Briddish." Christina pauses before eating a forkful of noodles. "The HIB or your cousin? Let's hear it."

"Dudette, you holding out on your fellow Esperteers is, like, cruel. What's with the HIB and your cousin?"

So I fill them in on the new situation with Joe, and how I've blown it so there's no point trying out any ESP on the HIB. Then I tell them about the repeated precognitive flashes I had about Naomi and Grandmother Gloria, and the good and bad outcomes. I tell them what I did to Naomi last night. *Had* to do to Naomi last night.

"So, you can see, I didn't have any choice. Dude's engagement could flip Naomi over the edge into a life of crime. Naomi's a lot more positive already. This morning when I got up for my early breakfast with Jessica, she came bouncing into the kitchen just as Jessica was making pancakes, because she wanted to go for a run around the garden."

Zak whistles. "I see what you mean, dudette, but I don't want anyone making me not love someone, even if it's unrequited love. What?" He turns to Christina when she digs him in the ribs. That's getting to be a habit, the rib-digging, but I think she means it in an affectionate way.

"How do you know it's unrequited?" Christina says to Zak, giving him another nudge.

"Really? I *knew* you had feelings for me." Zak sighs happily, but Christina raises her eyes to the ceiling and turns to me. "Men. But it would be irresponsible of you *not* to use your powers in a situation like that," Christina tells me approvingly, then her eyes narrow. "I still think you should fix the HIB. And your grandma."

"What do you mean about the Hot Italian Babe? You haven't had any precognitive flashes about her, have you?" April's eyes open wide. "She hasn't stolen Joe away from you, has she? I mean, it was a fight, not a breakup, right?"

"I still think you should add her to your hit list. For revenge."

Is Christina right? Should I compel the HIB to leave Joe alone? Like if I can't have him, neither can she? I wonder how I can compel her through the computer. If it worked through the TV, maybe over IM . . .

"What are you lot cooking up?" We all look up guiltily at Jessica and her tray of spaghetti and soda. Did she read our minds? Did she get even a flash of what I've been doing?

"Relax," she says with a laugh. "That was rhetorical. You were all concentrating so intently, I thought you might be plotting to take over the world or something."

"Who, us?" Christina is the picture of innocence.

"We were just helping Fiona with her boyfriend problems, because of the Italian competition," April improvises unhelpfully. I mean, I like Jessica and I think I'm getting to know her well, but I haven't exactly confided in her about Joe.

"You have Italian competition?" Jessica raises her eyebrows and places her tray down on the table. "Can I help?"

"The future's so bright, I hope you're wearing shades, Genius Girl," Will says when I answer my cell phone on Friday as Jessica and I drive home from boot camp. "We've found the missing link."

I'm glad he's got some good news, because I'm still not talking to Joe. I haven't had an e-mail from him since our fight on Wednesday. Then again, I haven't e-mailed him, either. Or Gina. Because I'm kind of scared that she'll confirm my worst fears.

"Yay. That's excellent news," I say to Will, because it is. "Are you allowed to say who the famous person is?"

"Not until I know for certain, sweetie."

"I understand. So what's next? I thought you didn't like approaching people directly."

"You're right, especially children. So this is what I need to do. This celebrity is known for her charity work, so under the guise of making a substantial donation I've had my people speak with her people. When I meet her I'll be able to assess if her powers are active or not, and take it from there."

"Fantastic," I say and relate the news to Jessica.

"There's a problem," Will says. "Her schedule has an opening on Sunday, which means—"

"—that you can't come home this weekend?"

"I'm really sorry."

"Don't worry about it for a moment," I say, mustering a cheery tone. "Everything's under control at Gulag Brown. And Jessica's taking Naomi and me to the mall tomorrow morning anyway, so we'll be too busy to miss you." How nice was it of Jessica to offer her services in my quest to forget my boyfriend troubles? If I actually still have a boyfriend. Jessica said it would do the three of us good to have a girly morning, no men allowed, but we were also planning to do a family dinner with Will. . . . I push my disappointment to the back of my mind—he's doing an important job.

Anyway, I asked Naomi last night when we were swimming, and she seemed really excited about it. Not a word about Dude, either, which is a good sign.

"There's the kicker." Will makes a big sigh. "I really need Jess to fly out here and attend the meeting with me—I need a woman's touch for this. As well as her ESP skills."

"Oh." I'm even more disappointed. But Will's quest is vital. "Never fear," I tell him. "We can go to the mall any old time." But you know what this also means? That Naomi and I will have to spend tonight being "improved" by Grandmother Gloria.

"Thanks for being so understanding, Fiona. I'll make it up to you." *No, I'll make it up to you,* I think, as Will asks me to tell Jessica about the situation, and for her to call him as soon as she's not driving. He's a safety superhero all the way.

I can manage the family. I've already started fixing it. How great will it be when Will gets home from dealing with his new espees and finds family harmony?

I am still thinking this as the car rolls down the drive and comes to a halt.

"Okay. See you Monday," Jessica says as I head toward the front door. "Don't worry too much about you-know-who."

"I'll try. Have a good trip." I wave good-bye as she drives away.

The house is so quiet, you could hear a pin drop. I get an odd prickly feeling as I climb the stairs. I'm getting to trust those prickly feelings, so I tread as gently and as quietly as possible, and when I get to the top, I pop my head around the side.

Grandmother Gloria is standing outside my bedroom. She's not actually facing my bedroom. She's not doing anything at all to suggest she might intend to charge in and, oh, take a hair from my hairbrush, but I don't make my presence known.

I get the same precognitive vision flash I had of her last week, featuring Will and me being led off in handcuffs by official-looking people. This reiterates my earlier conviction that I have to do something to fix her. But what?

I forget all about visions when there is a bang. It's loud enough to make me jump and spin around, and strong enough to rattle the windows. It makes Grandmother Gloria jump, too. It's coming from the basement.

"Your grandfather—" she says as she spots me, going pale.

"Grandfather Rick," I shout simultaneously and dash down the stairs, followed fairly closely by Grandmother Gloria.

"Oh, what has that silly man done now?" she says. I can tell she's anxious because she's running as fast as I am. "Oh, dear. Call for an ambulance, Fiona, and for the fire department."

We can see smoke coming from the closed basement door. This doesn't look good. Grandmother Gloria flings the door open. "Hold those phone calls, Fiona, we need to get your grandfather out of the basement. We need wet towels."

She pulls open the downstairs laundry cupboard and flings a pile of towels at me, and I head to the bathroom to drench them in water.

"It's all right, just a false alarm," Grandfather Rick's voice bellows through the basement door with the smoke. And then a very sooty Grandfather Rick emerges.

"Frederick!" Grandmother Gloria shrieks. "You're not dead!"

"I hope not." Grandfather Rick looks himself up and down. "I can't see any pearly gates. I'm just a bit singed around the edges."

And in an unusual lack of regard for her designer clothes, and an even more unusual display of affection, she hugs him. "Thank goodness, thank goodness, you had me worried, you silly man. What would I do without you? Are you hurt at all?" She steps back from him so she can inspect him more thoroughly.

"It looks far worse than it is," he says gruffly, patting her back.

"Shall I still call nine-one-one?" I ask.

"No, dear, there's no fire."

"Not this time," Grandmother Gloria admonishes him. "Who knows *who* we'll need to call, next time. The psychiatric unit? Look what you made me do to my clothes, you silly man."

And with that, Grandmother Gloria stalks off to change.

"Don't worry, she gets mad when she's frightened." Grandfather Rick's eyes follow her up the stairs. "She doesn't like any of her loved ones to be in any kind of danger."

"I know," I say.

"Even if it's just in danger of a sunburn." And then Grandfather Rick grins at me. It looks a bit odd, white teeth through a sooty face, and I can't help but laugh. He's not as absentminded as he lets on. "It's the sound," he explains to me. "It all carries into the basement."

In that moment I am so filled with affection for him that I know what to do.

I gather my will. I focus it.

"Are you all right, Fiona?"

I pull in more of my will. SPEND TIME WITH GRANDMOTHER GLORIA AND THE FAMILY, I think, and release my will. His eyes go blank for a moment, and then he grins at me again.

"I'm fine," I tell him. Then, when he blinks owlishly, "How are you?"

"You know, I feel great. Yes. I can't remember a time I felt better. I'd better clean myself up, put on something just a bit smarter than these old smoky clothes. I might even put on a dinner jacket. Your grandmother likes me in a dinner jacket," he says, winking at me.

He whistles a tune as he goes upstairs for a shower and change of clothes.

Progress.

"Anne, you've surpassed yourself with the chicken," Grandfather Rick booms jovially over dinner. Naomi glances across the table at me as if to say, "What's going on?" and I shrug and smile at her.

"And the asparagus. I don't remember when I last ate such tender asparagus. Do you, dear?" He turns to Grandmother Gloria. "In fact, I think I'll have a second helping. No, don't you worry, Anne, I'll serve everybody. Take the night off, you must be exhausted. Anybody else want more? Gloria, I must insist you have just a little more."

"Oh, Frederick, I can't—" Grandmother Gloria protests, but I can see that she's forgiven him for the explosion earlier, because she's smiling and fluttering her eyelashes at him as he takes her plate over to the food on the sideboard.

"Naomi? Fiona? Can I tempt you?" Grandfather Rick slides Grandmother Gloria's plate back in front of her. Her second helping is twice the size of her first.

"Yes, please, but I'll do it myself." I get up and walk over to the sideboard. This is excellent progress.

"I'm full, Grandfather." Naomi surprises me. She's only had the teeny-tiny portion we normally get.

"Whatever you feel like, my dear. So," Grandfather Rick adds as I take my place back at the table, "shall we do something as a family tonight? Fiona's been here over two weeks now and we mustn't neglect her."

"Usually, on Fridays, we listen to improving music and

read," Grandmother Gloria tells him, and I sigh. Loosen up, Grandmother Gloria. "We—we could do something else, if you like?"

"Excellent. I could do with some self-improvement. Music's good for the soul. Fiona, I believe your mother used to be in a band. Do you have any of her CDs with you? We'd love to listen, wouldn't we, Gloria? My, you look like Claire when she was your age. I was digging through some old photos in the basement earlier; I hope they didn't get ruined by the smoke. I'll pop downstairs and get them."

When he leaves, Grandmother Gloria, Naomi, and I look at one another.

"Grandfather Rick's in a good mood," Naomi comments.

MY GOOD POINTS, ACCORDING TO GRANDFATHER RICK AND GRANDMOTHER GLORIA, POST–FRIDAY EVENING'S FAMILY TIME

1. I have good dress sense. I was wearing black jeans with a white button-down shirt. I made a special effort to be tidy because of Grandmother Gloria's opinion on what the right clothes are for a Friday self-improvement evening. Grandfather Rick liked them, too, because he said that my outfit would look good on Naomi. Naomi got really enthusiastic about that, which reminded me about the mall trip. I asked Grandmother Gloria if it was okay for Steve to drive us. But I needn't have worried about getting to the mall, because Will had already called her about having a car available.

2. I have a very talented, successful mother. I didn't want to shock Grandmother Gloria too much with loud rock music, so I played them the acoustic, unplugged CD Mum cut with the Bliss Babes—with Mark Collingridge on guitar. Grandfather Rick insisted on me getting my laptop and loading her website. He was really impressed with all her achievements.
3. I am the spitting image of Aunt Claire when she was younger. While we listened to Mum and the Bliss Babes, Grandfather Rick got out all the photo albums, as well as the ones he brought up from the basement, and you could see right away that we are related. I think that alleviated Grandmother Gloria's fears about me being an imposter. I hope so anyway.

Talk about a successful Friday night. Apart from success with boyfriends, of course, I think as I load my e-mail. Oh. My. God. There's one from Joe. Shall I open it, or shall I ignore it? The subject sounds positive. . . .

To: "Fiona Blount" <MarieCurieGirl@bluesky.com>
From: "Joe Summers" <OccamsRazor@sciencenet.com>
Subject: Top-Secret Rendezvous

Through very devious means (sneaking off to the electronics store by myself this morning, before anyone could ask where I was going, and could they come, too?), I have acquired a webcam so that I can make a date with my beautiful girlfriend and see her sweet face while I speak with her (I miss that sweet face). Because, Fiona, we do need to speak.

I didn't mention Isabella because, frankly, she's a nuisance, and I didn't want you to get the wrong idea. Which you did, because like a fool I thought if I ignored Isabella she'd go away. I've thought about it some more and I know if you were here instead of me, and Brian was sending me photos of you with a Hot Italian Guy, I'd be completely baffled if you didn't mention him, either. I'm sorry. ☹

So about that date. Tomorrow? Daytime for me is impossible, but Dr. Fiori's family is throwing us a going-away party tomorrow night (*he* is great, even if his daughter's loony, so I can't not go). I think we'll be back here at the apartment by 11 p.m. because the flight home the next day is really early. How about midnight my time, 6 p.m. in the evening your time?

Love,
Your Idiot Boyfriend XX

PS. Picture of hot calendar-worthy sorry nerd attached.

PPS. 狂気を好む

Love? And I'm his beautiful girlfriend? He's not planning on ditching me for the HIB. Yay! I open Joe's photo.

He's frowning in a sad kind of way. I smile and check out his Japanese message.

To: "Joe Summers" <OccamsRazor@sciencenet.com>

From: "Fiona Blount" <MarieCurieGirl@bluesky.com>

Subject: Re: Top-Secret Rendezvous

It's a date! I'm sorry, too. It wasn't you I didn't trust, it was the HIB.

<<OccamsRazor@sciencenet.com said: 狂気を好む>>

You like the lunatic? I certainly do like the lunatic, LOL.

"I can't remember the last time I had this much fun," Naomi tells me as we wander through the mall the next day.

Aunt Claire stops to check out a cute T-shirt. "Me, neither. It's been too long since we had some mother-daughter time. How about this one, Naomi? It's made from fair-trade cotton, of course," she adds. "It's important not to purchase clothes that have been created by the sweat of slave-labor conditions."

Yes, Aunt Claire is with us, too. Her presence is all due to the new, improved Grandfather Rick.

This morning, as he was on his way to breakfast, Aunt Claire was dashing through the hall on her way to do some important bird-sanctuary work at the Meadowlands. Grandfather Rick intercepted her. I saw the whole thing, because I was on my way to breakfast, too.

"Claire, Claire, you haven't had breakfast, yet. The birds can wait. Come, my dear, let's have a real family breakfast. You've hardly seen Naomi since she came back from Florida."

I thought it was very diplomatic of Grandfather Rick not to mention Naomi's dad.

"Well—I suppose I could—"

"Excellent, that's all settled." Before she could change her mind, Grandfather Rick steered her into the dining room, pushed his daughter into a seat, and got some toast for her.

In the midst of eating huge quantities of toast, he managed to talk practically nonstop.

"While you gals are on your spending spree, I'm taking your grandmother to the golf club. No argument," he said, smiling at Grandmother Gloria.

"Oh." Grandmother Gloria's face lost all its sharp angles. "Why, Frederick, dear, it's so long since we played a few rounds. Years."

"That's what I thought, so it's time to put that straight. The exercise will be great, and don't you fuss for a minute about skin cancer, we'll make sure we sunblock up. Then we can have a nice lunch at the Cricketers." Then, "You girls got enough money?" He stood up and took his wallet out of his pocket. "Here you go," he said, holding out two fifty-dollar notes to me and Naomi. "Buy something nice on me."

"I'm fine, I have money, but it's terribly sweet of you," I told him, a bit embarrassed. I think Naomi was reluctant to take it, too.

"Come on, girls, when do I ever treat you? Take this as a down payment for future spoiling-by-grandfather."

Instinctively, we both glanced at Grandmother Gloria, but she was fairly sphinxlike. Although in a soft way, still no sharp angles. That must be where Will gets it—his sphinxlike inscrutability.

"The usual response is, 'Thank you very much,'" Grandmother Gloria said. So that's what we said and took the money. Then, "Keep it somewhere safe, because there are so many thieves around these days. And don't loiter in any parts of the parking lot that don't have security—you hear such terrible tales, terrible tales."

Aunt Claire smiled benignly. "It's so nice to have the family together. It's a shame Will's not here, too." It seemed like Grandfather Rick's amiable rambling was rubbing off on her.

Privately, I thought it was kind of a good thing Will *wasn't* there, because this meant that they could be functional and happy together, even if he was away on business. I didn't say that, of course.

"Claire, you should go with them." Grandfather Rick took another fifty-dollar bill out of his wallet. "You deserve to take some time out—you do so much for other people that you forget about yourself."

"I suppose—" Aunt Claire began.

"I won't take no for an answer," Grandfather Rick steamrollered over her again. "All my girls deserve a little spoiling."

So that was that. Within a half hour Grandfather Rick had bundled the three of us into Aunt Claire's car, and here we are.

"Mom, this would be so great with your skirt." Naomi pulls out a beige jacket in DKNY.

"Oh, no—"

"Oh, yes." Naomi giggles and holds it out. Aunt Claire tries it on. Naomi's right. Aunt Claire looks at herself in the mirror as if she can't remember what she looks like.

In the end, I buy two pink Ts—one baby-pink one, with white trim and a bow in the middle (to remind Joe that I'm a girl as well as a brain), and a deep rose one with black trim. Naomi told me it was "edgy."

She's really coming out of her shell!

Over lunch with Aunt Claire, Naomi doesn't eat anything, though. She just has a cappuccino.

"Upset stomach," she tells us.

"You poor thing," Aunt Claire says. "There's nothing worse."

She must be feeling bad. She didn't eat anything at breakfast, either.

It's time!

My hair is flicky, my lips are glossy, and I'm wearing my new baby-pink T.

Joe said he'd call me as soon as the coast was clear. So here I am, in my bedroom, waiting for *his call.*

I nearly jump out of my skin when the Skype phone rings. I click the green phone button.

"Hi," I say, almost shyly, because I'm a bit nervous.

"Fiona, at last, I thought I'd never get away. When we left, the Fioris came with us. They're all still in the living room, but I had to sneak off and see you."

Then the video pops up and I can see him. Not all six feet of him, but his face and shoulders. That sweet face and hazel eyes smattered with little green flecks. His hair has grown a bit; it's almost in his eyes. And it looks more golden brown than ever. It must be that strong Italian sun.

"You look lovely," we both say at the same time. And laugh. From the way he's looking at me, I don't think he's seeing me as just a brain.

"God, Fiona, I've missed you," he says, running his hand through his bangs to push them off his forehead. "It's been great over here, apart from my—problem—I'm really sorry about that."

"I shouldn't have gotten upset. I should have known there'd be a rational explanation. I've missed you, too."

Before he can tell me about his trouble with the HIB, I hear voices in the background. Two voices. More voices. Then,

"Surprise!"

Brian, Gina, and Peaceflower come into the shot. And an Italian boy who I think must be Vespa Boy.

They're all talking at once so it's hard to make them out. I have to say that Joe looks annoyed. I feel pretty annoyed, too. It was supposed to be just me and Joe. Then I calm myself down. These are my friends. I wave at the webcam and they all wave back.

Once they settle down, I can hear them individually. Kind of.

"We thought it would be fun to crash your private party." Brian grins at me, and I can't stay mad at him. He's a bit of a clown but a nice one.

Gina doesn't look very happy, though.

"Hi, Gina," I call to her, to make her feel better. "It's great to see you all."

"It's lovely to see you, too," Gina says, then, "This wasn't really my idea, I thought you and Joe should have a bit of privacy. But someone"—she clunks Brian on the ear—"let the cat out of the bag."

"Peaceflower, how do you like Italy?" I ask.

"Oh, Fiona, *belissima*, Fiona," Peaceflower says to me. "Here is my one true love, Giovanni." Vespa Boy waves. "It's nice to see you, even though I'm sure you want to be alone with your own one true love." I redden a bit at that and glance at Joe. He gives me the ghost of a smile.

"It's okay, you can blame me for the crashing date," comes a husky, sexy voice, and then Isabella slithers into view. She is more beautiful in real life than in her photos. She slides one of her arms over Joe's shoulders, and she looks so comfortable like that I can't help but wonder if Joe wasn't telling the whole truth. If maybe she's less of a nuisance to him than he led me to believe. "I am so happy to meet you, Fiona, your friends have told me much about you. But as you see, I am looking after them well. And looking after your Joe well, too."

I plaster a smile to my face. I can see that Joe is trying, gently, to remove her arm, which comforts me. But she's like a limpet on a rock!

Or maybe he's not really trying that hard because he doesn't want her arm to go anywhere?

"I take your lovely friends to see all the sights of Roma."

I am so confused and cross that I start to gather my will. I am going to fix the Hot Italian Babe so that she leaves my boyfriend alone.

"I'll e-mail you, Fiona," Gina states firmly.

The room fills with more people and it gets harder to hear what individuals are saying.

"Um, Isabella," Joe mutters, tugging at her arm.

I focus my will. GET AWAY FROM MY BOYFRIEND, I think, as I prepare to release my will on her. Then I stop. Joe's eyes are speaking volumes to me. It's clear that he's truly not even remotely interested in the HIB.

He really didn't want me to get the wrong impression. He didn't want me worrying for no reason at all. I release my unused will into the universe, bit by bit.

"Um, Fiona." His eyebrows are furrowed since I've been so quiet and I smile reassuringly.

"Oh, Joe, I can see what you mean about the HIB," I speak loudly into my mike. I think the whole room hears me, because there's a dip in the noise volume. "Don't worry. I get it. I trust you. It's a bit, um, like having your own barnacle, isn't it?"

Joe laughs with relief.

Isabella looks confused, like she thinks maybe we're talking about her but isn't totally sure.

We hung up after that, because it's just too hard to speak to so many people at the same time. As we disconnected, I made the fingers-to-keyboard sign to Joe and he nodded.

True to her word, Gina e-mails me straightaway.

To: "Fiona Blount" <MarieCurieGirl@bluesky.com>
From: "Gina Duffy" <Feminista@bluesky.com>
Subject: That girl

I'm sorry, Fiona, I just didn't see it coming. You know what I'm like sometimes. I thought she treated all the boys like that. I thought she was nice, at first.

I thought it was an Italian thing. Then when I got worried I didn't know what to say to you. Joe was always very impersonal with her and kept her at arm's length. But you can see how determined she is.

I tried to hint at it with the last set of photos I sent to you. I think you got it.

Your friend always XX

I e-mail Gina right back to tell her not to worry anymore. Because I'm not. Everything's right on track!

Also, you know Wilkon, the company the HIB thought I should invest in? Its CEO has been arrested for fraud, and the share prices have plummeted.

The HIB isn't as smart as she thinks she is.

"Everything's perfectly fine." I smile at Will and Jessica via Skype. "We're having a great time." It's true, I have fixed the family!

"No . . . little problems with anybody in particular?" Jessica asks me. "Even teeny-weeny ones?"

"Nope. Aunt Claire took us to the mall yesterday, and when we got back Grandfather Rick decided that we should all go out to dinner," I tell them both.

"Claire went to the mall?" Will shakes his head in disbelief, and I want to laugh. He's going to be so thrilled with all the positive changes.

"Yes. She even came with us into Manhattan today. Grandmother Gloria spent so much money in Bloomingdale's, but not on herself—on Aunt Claire, Naomi, and me. She might not fully understand the concept of living a little dangerously, but she certainly knows how to spend dangerously, especially at the encouragement of Grandfather Rick."

Will shakes his head again. "You're having quite the positive effect on the family." If only he knew.

"Of course she has a positive effect, she's lovely," Jessica jumps in, and I get the warm fuzzies in the pit of my stomach.

Then, because they haven't said anything about the celeb and family espees, I ask, "How did it go on your end today?"

"Do you want to tell it, or shall I?" Will asks Jessica.

"Oh, let me, because you're too modest to describe your superherodom," Jessica teases him, then looks back at me through the webcam. "Your dad was his charming, suave self, of course. After we'd had coffee and chatted with the megastar, he loaded Funktech's website on his laptop, on the pretext of wanting to show her some figures about Africa and where he thought his donation could be well spent.

"Anyway, he loaded the 'Meet the CEO' page with the hidden message, and, boy, did she jump when she heard that hidden message."

"It scared the bejeebers out of me the first few times." I laugh. "Go on."

"Once she'd calmed down and we showed her a few, you know, handy tricks, she let us test her. She thought she was alone, so she was relieved to discover she's not. She's a really strong empath. It explains why she's such a fabulous actress—she can really feel the characters she plays."

"Am I allowed to know who she is?"

"Top secret." Will touches the side of his nose.

"Of course. I promise never to utter her name in connection with ESP," I vow. *Wow,* I think, when Jessica says the name. *Her?* That makes sense. "She's one of the most talented actresses in the world!"

"Her daughters also tested quite strongly. The older girl was a bit standoffish at first," Jessica says. "But once her mother convinced her it would be okay, she was less scared."

"What happens now? I mean, they're too late for boot camp this time around."

"Seeing as who she is, and that we're dealing with three espees, two who are developing their skills at a younger age," Will begins, "we're going to stay with them this week and give them some training. We're bringing over a few other espees, too."

I guess my smile must have faltered a little (the problem with Skype!) because Will says, "Don't worry, Fiona," looking earnestly at me. "We'll both be back by next weekend, pinky swear." He holds out his pinky to touch his webcam, and I put my pinky against mine.

"Parental Unit, you do realize that I'm too old for this pinky stuff, don't you?"

"I'm allowed. Hmm. Parental Unit. I like that." So do I. I'm really starting to think of him as my dad, now. Then a thought occurs to me.

"How will I get to boot camp this week?"

"I've spoken to Miss Bird. She'll be driving you back and forth."

Will really thinks of everything.

It seems like I don't know a thing, though.

What is wrong with Z'Aktagnan and the other two Esperteers today?

"What?" I mouth silently to Zak in the middle of ESP theory as he leans forward from the other side of Christina and gives me yet another meaningful look. Instead of answering me he looks to Christina for help.

"Briddish, we may have a small problem," Christina whispers to me through the side of her mouth.

"What do you mean? What kind of problem?" I whisper back as Sean tells Cristobel Lantigue that quantum theory is only a theory, according to his mother, and not proven, and Cristobel explains that in science "theory" means something quite different from the way it's used in common speech.

"You didn't do any more funny stuff over the weekend, did you?" April whispers, her expression worried.

"What do you mean by funny stuff?" I'm completely confused.

"Did you watch any TV?" Christina asks meaningfully.

"No." It was way too busy for TV.

"Can't tell you now; we need to wait until break time." Christina shakes her head. I look back from Christina to April. How mysterious.

"In science, theory is used to describe the results of mounds of observable and empirical evidence," Cristobel drones on in her dry, dusty voice.

Strange looks and equally strange behavior *are* observable evidence, and I am jumping to the conclusion that maybe somebody else knows about my little foray into the world of ESP compulsion. Oh, no!

"Did someone, you know, find out?" I whisper to Christina. She shakes her head again. Okay, so what else could the trouble be?

"Although quantum mechanics is still hypothetical, many of its unproven data are used in technology like—" Cristobel pauses midflow. "April, Christina, Fiona—you want to share the uses, because it seems you must know this already since you're chatting instead of paying attention. Unless you'd like to share your conversation with us all?"

"It's used in cell phones, computers, and satellite navigation systems," Christina returns, without batting an eyelid.

I have to wait until after focus and shielding before I find out what's going on.

"There's something you need to see in the TV room, dudette," Zak says as soon as we break from lessons for fifteen minutes.

"Shields up securely, everybody?" Christina warns us all, glancing around the corridor. We nod in tandem.

When we duck into the TV room, Zak extends his additional safety shield over us and switches on *The Apartment.*

"I fink it's perfectly reasonable that everybody should maintain high standards of hygiene," Dude, resplendent in yellow rubber gloves and an apron, is telling Peter, one of his fellow inhabitants. "Look, man, it just isn't fair if I have to do everyfink mysewf. See your name on vis list? You're down for cleaning the bathroom today, so why 'aven't you done it?"

"Chill out, I cleaned it already," Peter tries to soothe him. Dude grabs him by the arm and marches him to the bathroom.

"You call vis clean? Clean?" Dude sighs loudly and looks into the camera. "Vey say if you want a job done right, you have to do it yer own bloody self."

I'd call it clean. From this side of the camera it looks fairly spotless.

"Dude, what's come over you? Cleaning the house at all times, day and night? That's not normal, man."

"That's because I'm living wiv a group of pigs," Dude shrieks and grabs a bottle of bleach.

Peter shrugs and retreats to another room.

Oh. My. God.

"Do you think this has anything to do with me you-know-what-ing him?" I look anxiously at Z'Aktagnan and my two Esperteers.

"Dudette, he had the same reaction yesterday when Jenna did the vacuuming. And Letitia and the windows." Zak hasn't really answered my question.

"They got so mad at him that they told him if he could do a better job than them, then he should do it himself," April chimes in. "Unfortunately, he took them at their word. He's driving everybody nuts with his never-ending vacuuming and polishing and dusting." April hasn't really answered my question, either.

"Yes, I think this has something to do with you you-know-what-ing him." Christina doesn't beat around the bush. "I guess you just used too much power on him." Then she gets an even more concerned look on her face. "How's your cousin doing?"

"She's—" I'm about to say "fine," but I hesitate. I mean, she *is* fine, she's been joining in with the family stuff this weekend, and she seemed all perky and happy. But . . .

"Doing anything strange?" Christina prods me.

"I don't remember her eating very much all weekend. She *has* eaten, but only little bits."

"Maybe she's not hungry," April suggests. "I go through periods of time when I'm not hungry."

"Dudette, you didn't try out any more little character tweaks, did you? It was just your cousin and the Dude Mann dude?"

"Well. There was the incident with my grandfather. . . ." I tell them about it and what Grandfather Rick's been like all weekend.

"I'm sure it will be fine, Briddish," Christina says when I've finished. She doesn't look very sure about it, though. Neither do Zak and April.

Okay. I'm worried that I've caused Naomi to become anorexic.

At dinner tonight, while Grandfather Rick was telling us all about the last vacation he and Grandmother Gloria took—to the Grand Canyon—and wouldn't it be great if we all took a vacation together before I left for England, and ran through a possible list of places he thought we could go, and Grandmother Gloria said how about somewhere nice and safe like Boston, nobody but me noticed Naomi not eating.

I decide to call Mum. Actually, she sounded a bit odd the last time I spoke to her, last week. I've been meaning to call, but with fixing the family it slipped my mind. Her e-mails are all fun and full of what she's up to, but it will be great to actually speak to her.

"What would you do if you thought someone was on the verge of developing an eating disorder?"

"Well, that's a good opening line. Who has an eating disorder? Not you, I hope!" Mum says.

"No, just—just someone at boot camp." I hate not telling Mum the truth, but if I say it's Naomi she'll be on the telephone to Parental Unit Will before I can count to ten.

"Let me see what Wiki has to say about it," she says. "Has this person noticeably lost weight?"

"Um, no." It's only been a few days.

"Oh, so that rules out involuntary hospital treatment. It says here that family therapy is one of the most effective treatments for adolescents, blah, blah, blah, what else. Oh, yes. Forty percent of those affected are girls between the ages of fifteen and nineteen. I'm guessing this person falls into that category."

"Yes."

"Maybe you should tell an authority figure at science camp."

"Maybe I'm just overreacting. I mean, she's only missed a few meals. That I know about anyway. So, how are you and Mark and Daphne Kat?" I ask to change the subject.

"Mark's fine, and Daphne Kat loves only me now, mwahahaha, O provider of General Tso's Chicken," Mum teases me. "No, really, she's still sleeping exclusively on your bed. Sharon's been popping in every lunchtime to give her a bit of company."

"Daphne Kat's normally okay by herself when I'm at school," I say, because Sharon popping in that often sounds odd. "What gives?"

Mum sighs. "I wasn't sure I should tell you, but Daphne Kat had to have a little operation after you left. She swallowed the top from a pen. But she's okay, now, chasing pens around the house like the mad cat we know and love. Don't worry—I'm careful to remove the caps first."

Before I can say anything about poor Daphne Kat, I hear Grandfather Rick at my bedroom door. "Fiona? You coming down to play cards with the rest of the family? I want to teach you the traditional Brown game of Bag."

"I heard that. You go, Fabulous Fiona, we'll catch up later in the week."

"You're sure she's all right?"

"Positive, now go!"

"Coming," I say to Grandfather Rick.

"Zoe, you can't be too careful about cooker hygiene," Dude tells the love of his life. "You've left some marks, luv, look."

"You know what, Dude? I liked you better before. You can take your metaphorical engagement ring and shove it you-know-where," Zoe yells at him, pulls off her rubber gloves, and throws them in his face.

"Zoe, luv, you can't mean that. Every couple has lover's tiffs." Dude follows her to her bedroom. She slams the door in his face. Dude turns to the camera. "She'll get over it when she's had a bit of time to fink it through. I'll clean the cooker mysewf."

"Do you think he's getting worse?" I ask Zak, Christina, and April the next day at lunchtime when we sneak into the TV room.

"I heard he's trying to pull his book, *My Life So Far*, because he says that the mad, bad, and rude life depicted in the book isn't the Dude Mann dude he is now," Zak tells me.

"I bet that's going down well with his publisher," Christina remarks drily. "He still claims to be speaking to the disenfranchised, material youth."

"They're not talking back." April shakes her head. "I wouldn't be surprised if he gets voted off the show next."

"I've ruined his career," I wail. "Haven't I?"

I look around at my friends. "No, dudette, maybe not his *whole* career. He could always take up home improvement, instead. Like a makeover show."

"Or maybe he could get another book deal for a self-help guide," April hypothesizes.

"Thank you, April, for your positivity, but tell it like it is."

I turn to Christina, who says, "How's your grandpa? He showing any obsessive signs?"

"Well, he was already a bit obsessive," I say, remembering how he hardly came up from the basement earlier in my visit. "So, not yet."

Although maybe just a bit.

I needn't worry about that secret DNA test I saw in Grandmother Gloria's precognitive moment. The way things are now she doesn't have time for sneaking into my room. She has a permanently haunted look on her face.

I mean, I thought I was doing the right thing giving Grandmother Gloria her heart's desire—that Grandfather Rick spend time with her—but that's backfired, too. It was fine at first—it was cute when he wanted to take her to lunch, meet her for coffee, come to all the family meals on time, and wanted us all to join in with family stuff. But now he follows her around the house like a puppy dog, and he never stops talking.

I seem to have given him a new obsession.

I have been here three weeks today, and look what havoc I've caused, I think, as I eat a cheese sandwich in the kitchen after boot camp.

I look up when Grandmother Gloria comes rushing into the room. She pauses right in the middle of the kitchen as if she's forgotten what she came for.

"Can I get you something, Mrs. Brown?" Anne asks her gently.

"A Bloody Mary would be nice," Grandmother Gloria says just a bit hysterically, then she laughs as she hears Grandfather Rick calling out her name. "Make that a double." When she sees the flustered expression on Anne's face, she adds, "It's okay, Anne, that was a joke."

"Um, I think he means well. Maybe he just wants to get out of his basement more. Um, and spend a bit of time with the family," I say, feeling guilty.

"You're right." Grandmother Gloria sits opposite me, puts her elbow on the table, and rests her chin on it. And just as I'm sure the conversation is over because it's been longer than all of our previous ones (unless they involve me being chastised), she continues. "You know, I really wanted Grandfather Frederick to spend more time upstairs. I guess that saying, 'Be careful what you wish for because you might get it' is true, after all. I do want us to spend time together, but tonight it's the ladies' club meeting, and he wants to come with me. All day every day is just too much for a person."

Oh, I wish I'd never meddled in the first place.

"Do you want me to distract him while you make your escape? I could, you know, see if he's interested in showing me his inventions." Not that he's invented anything since last Friday when I befuddled his head.

"Would you?" She looks at me with an expression I don't recognize. I think it's warmth. Or appreciation. Or maybe both.

"Of course." *Seeing as it's my fault in the first place,* I nearly add, but don't.

"That's kind of you, Fiona," Grandmother Gloria says, touching my arm. "I'm sorry I wasn't more welcoming when you first arrived; it was the shock of finding out Will had a daughter."

"I completely understand. You were looking out for his best interests. For all you knew I could be a scheming money-digger." Grandmother Gloria blushes with embarrassment when I say that, which is not what I intended, so I rush to add, "Not that you thought that, of course. Okay, wish me luck with Grandfather Rick."

I put down my cheese sandwich and walk into the hall.

"Have you seen your grandma, Fiona?" Grandfather Rick is all dressed up in a suit and tie.

"You look lovely, today."

"Thank you, my dear." He pats me on the shoulder. "You should always make an effort, especially when you're stepping out with the most beautiful woman in the world."

How sweet is that?

"I thought tonight was supposed to be just ladies," I prompt him. "How about showing me some of your newest inventions? In fact, I want you to show me every single last one of them and tell me how they work." I deserve to suffer.

"That's very good of you, but can I take a rain check on that? I'll fit right in with those ladies—I can really liven them up with a few of my jokes and stories of the old days, when we weren't so rich and posh. Kinda keeps an old fella grounded in reality. Gloria," he shouts out. "Where are you, my sweetness? I've checked everywhere else; she must be in the kitchen."

"Here I am, Frederick." Grandmother Gloria gives me a defeated little smile as she comes into the hallway. "I just think this will be so boring for you."

"I'm never bored when you're around." Then he kisses her on the cheek. "Don't wait up for us," he says to me. "I'm taking your grandma for a light surprise supper afterward. Oh, my, I let the cat out of the bag. It was supposed to be a secret."

"I appreciate the sentiment, Frederick." Grandmother Gloria sighs as they go out the front door. "But you don't have to surprise me so very often."

I sigh, too, and head up to check on Naomi. I run smack into Aunt Claire, who is hiding on the stairs.

"Have they gone?" she asks me, with a haunted expression much like Grandmother Gloria wore just now. "I can't step out of the door when Dad's around. He's like a maniac family man, all 'Let's play cards like a real family,' or 'Let's watch a movie together.' It's kind of nice, but it's a bit too much at times."

"It's safe," I assure her. Then, "Aunt Claire, have you noticed that Naomi's not been eating very much, recently?"

"Hasn't she? I guess I haven't been paying proper attention. Thanks for pointing that out to me, I'll be sure to keep an eye on her. It's so hard being a teen—all the traps girls can fall into in modern life."

"I'm just about to see if she wants to swim with me."

"You've been a good influence on this family, Fiona."

No, I haven't. I've been the very worst kind of influence.

When I knock on Naomi's door, I notice the chaos of paper and materials in her bedroom.

"It's like I've been divinely inspired to create," she tells me. "Look at all these designs. This is my favorite," she says, showing me a design for a swimsuit. Cut high on the leg, low at the top, it features a skinny model.

"It's great," I tell her. "But wouldn't it look better if you had a, you know, model who had a bit more flesh on her?"

"Oh, no," Naomi tells me. "You can never be too skinny."

"That's not what you said last week."

"That was the old me talking," she says gaily as she grabs her towel. "That's last week's news. I don't mean really skinny, just slim like this model. It can't hurt to be smaller than my current size ten, especially since I want to model my own creations. Come on, I want to do at least fifty laps in the pool."

Gina's online when I switch on my laptop. What's a girl to do when she's a complete and utter failure, except tell her best friend?

MarieCurieGirl to Feminista: Here are three wishes I will never make again. That certain TV celebrities would become more responsible citizens. That my cousin would forget about Dude and make the most of herself. That my grandfather would spend more time with the family. I bet you can turn at least one of those wishes into a known disaster (if you watch the news).

Feminista to MarieCurieGirl: OMG, do U mean who I think U mean 4 wish 1?

MarieCurieGirl to Feminista: Yes. The other two wishes worked out just as well.

Feminista to MarieCurieGirl: Oh, no ☹. Poor U.

Maybe the wishes will wear off as per Melissa Stevens and the zombification?

MarieCurieGirl to Feminista: Aw, thank you for that. You're a good friend, but what do I do if they don't?

Feminista to MarieCurieGirl: Tell ur dad.

MarieCurieGirl to Feminista: I meant to *help* him, to *fix* things, not cause *more* trouble.

Feminista to MarieCurieGirl: Sometimes it's good to rely on others. To ask for help. Don't take this the wrong way, but U R only 14. U don't have to get everything right all the time.

Gina's very wise. Because look what happens when I try to manage everything myself.

MarieCurieGirl to Feminista: Enough about me. What's it like to be home? Wish I were there instead of in hot water.

Feminista to MarieCurieGirl: It's great to be home ☺. Italy was lovely, apart from she-who-will-never-be-mentioned-again. Oh, Peaceflower's going to die of separation from Giovanni, so she says. She's enrolling in Italian classes and she's planning to go over and see him again. Kieran's missed me—he's practically been here every day since Sunday evening when we got home. Isn't that minty?

MarieCurieGirl to Feminista: Minty's the word. Kieran knows a good thing when he sees it. ☺ Is Joe there right now?

Feminista to MarieCurieGirl: No, he's at home. Said he had something important to do tonight???

As I am wondering what that something important is, there is a knock on my door, right at that moment. It's Anne.

"There's someone named Joe on the phone for you," she tells me, holding out the landline. My heart thuds in my chest.

MarieCurieGirl to Feminista: Back later. Love calls!

"Hi, you," I say, smiling. I have butterflies in my stomach.

"Hi, yourself. Am I calling at a good time?"

"You can call me any time you want," I flirt. "But why didn't you just call my cell phone?"

"I wanted to make sure there wouldn't be any reception problems or patches where we couldn't hear each other. So I got the number from your mum and am taking full advantage of the cheap international plan Dad found."

How great is that?

"Marie Curie Girl, I want you to do something for me. But you can't ask any questions. You'll love this. Do you trust me?"

"I'm intrigued." Also less sad about my latest ESP disasters, due to talking to Joe.

"That's the idea, I'm an intriguing kind of guy."

"You got that one right."

"Look, I want you to go to one of the squillions of rooms in your dad's mansion where there's a TV and turn it on."

"Which one? Um, the one in the living room or the one in the kitchen?" Now I'm confused. What does the TV have to do with anything?

"Any is fine. Just trust me, okay?"

"Okay," I say, because I do. Trust him. "I'm heading down the grand staircase. I'm turning into the huge, elaborate hall featuring the most ornate chandelier you could ever lay your eyes on. I am now walking into the *Chambre Marie Antoinette*. That's the Marie Antoinette living room to you and me."

"I love it when you talk French to me." I can hear the smile in Joe's voice as he says this. "I know I'm not very good at vocalizing, you know, mushy stuff. . . ." He trails off.

"You're actually getting very good at it."

"You think? Are you at the TV yet?"

"Yes." I wish he'd continued, instead of trailing off. I could use the lift. What was he going to say to me?

"I want you to switch it on and tune in to an empty channel—one with static. I know this sounds crazy, but you'll see why in a minute."

I will?

"Okay," I say, confused. "Plenty of static. Why are we doing this?"

"I have my TV switched on to static, too. Do you know what this means, Fiona? Because you're very smart and you usually get me straightaway."

Not this time, I don't. But before I can reply, Joe steps into the void.

"Some of that static on your screen is ancient microwaves—so ancient that they date back to the beginning of the universe. To the Big Bang itself. And, Fiona, that's how I feel about . . ." That last word comes out very choked, and I understand instantly what he's saying.

"Are you, um, saying that you missed me for thirteen and a half billion years?" I whisper into the phone.

"Exactly that, give or take a few extra billion," he says, and his voice is still odd. I know that this stuff is hard for boys, but sometimes a girl needs to hear it for herself, so I stay quiet and wait for him to go on. "All of that time, the universe has been expanding, everything has been getting so far apart. That static is a reminder that it was together, once. So, any time you feel like you're missing me or something—because I'm missing you a lot—I want you to turn on the static and call me, and then we can watch the beginning of the universe together. Is that a deal?"

"Definitely!" Sometimes microwaves can be more romantic than the L-word.

"And by the way, O R R L M C G," Joe says, and my heart flips even more. See, when we were first getting together we played this letter game. Each of us would come up with a set of letters, and the other person had to guess what they meant.

That time, the letters meant Occam's Razor Really Likes Marie Curie Girl.

"I R T F," I say, which means I Reciprocate That Feeling.

"And the L stands for a lot more than plain old like," Joe says.

"For me, too," I tell him. "That's definitely good mush."

Then, after a pause, he asks, "Fiona, are you okay? You're a bit quiet. Is anything wrong?"

"You're getting really good at knowing how I feel," I tell him as a tear escapes and slips down my cheek. "I did something a bit stupid, I can't really say what it is, and now I have to sort it out."

"Nothing can be *that* terrible," he reassures me. "Can't your dad help you out with it?"

"I hope so," I answer.

I really hope so.

Chapter 17

"Fiona, I think your grandfather has some kind of degenerative brain disease," Grandmother Gloria tells me when she comes into the kitchen early on Friday morning as I am eating my solitary toast before boot camp.

"I don't think so," I say as instant guilt floods me. "He's more the opposite of degenerative—he's more like *re*generative," I babble on, dropping my toast onto my plate. It tastes like cardboard, anyway.

"Ever since the blast he hasn't been himself." She lowers herself into the seat beside me. "I need to get him to a doctor."

Then I notice that Grandmother Gloria isn't as meticulously groomed as she usually is. She's wearing a nightgown and not a scrap of makeup. I am so surprised you could knock me off my chair with a puff of breath. She looks—more human.

"Well," I begin, playing for time. "It's Friday. Why not wait until Monday? Maybe it's the shock of the blast. Yes, I think it's just the shock of the blast. You should talk to Will when he gets home tonight, he'll know what to do. I think Grandfather Rick's going to be just fine. You'll see." I cross my fingers under the table as I say that last part. I mean, can my mistakes be fixed?

Grandmother reaches across and pats my arm. She actually *touches* me for the second time this week.

"You're a good girl, Fiona." I feel even *more* terrible at that. "But what if it's a brain tumor? They can cause people to become better for a little while, then they regress."

"Oh, I don't think it's a brain tumor," I say a little too cheerfully. "Um, do you want some coffee? I'll, um, make us some coffee." I leap up because I need to do something. At that moment Naomi comes jogging into the kitchen. From outside the house. I glance at my watch. It's only six thirty.

"Morning, everyone," she says as she slows down and begins some stretching exercises. "It's a great day for a run through the grounds. All that fresh air, all that great exercise. I feel like a new woman—like a budding supermodel."

"Naomi, do you want some toast? Because it's no trouble. You should have something to eat after all that exercise," I say. "And breakfast is the most important meal of the day." I've been trying to tempt her at each mealtime, but her eating hasn't improved any, and I'm sure she looks thinner this week.

"No thanks, I'll get some later," she says over her shoulder as she heads to the hall. "I need to shower and get dressed first. I have a lot of work to do today on my new collection."

"I'm beginning to think somebody else has a *re*generative disease, too," Grandmother Gloria says with a laugh, and I laugh with her, but not because the situation is funny. It's the first time I've ever heard her crack a joke. Even under bad circumstances, although she doesn't know what they are.

"Fiona, can I speak with you, please?" Miss Bird asks me as the bell rings for lunch.

My stomach whooshes, just like it does in the speedy elevator from the ground floor to this subterranean part of the building. Has she guessed what I did?

"We'll wait outside for you, dudette," Zak says.

"See you in five." Christina gives me a nod.

"Or sooner, if Miss Bird only wants a quick word," April adds encouragingly.

Once Sean, Farah, and Mehreen have also left, Miss Bird closes the door and indicates that I should sit down. My shield is up and firmly in place, just in case of an incriminating thought that Miss Bird might read in my mind.

"Is something bothering you, dear? You haven't been as focused as usual for the last few days. You had the art of levitation down to a fine art, nearly, so what was that crashing table about just now?"

"Oh, I'm fine, Miss Bird," I say quickly.

"Mr. Rafaelle didn't think so in compulsion class. He said you couldn't successfully compel April to imitate a chicken." She's right. I was a total beginner; everybody else in the class did both lessons perfectly.

"I think I'm just missing my dad, having only just found him, and that kind of stuff. I'll be fine when he gets home tonight." That last part might be wrong. I may never be fine again.

"You know you can talk to me, if you need to?" I nod. "Okay, dear," she says with a sigh. "Run along with your friends. And

Fiona." I pause at the door. "Your shield feels very strong, despite your lack of focus in class this week. Neither I, nor any other member of staff, would ever read your mind without your explicit agreement, you know."

"What gives?" Zak asks me as soon as I get into the corridor. I shake my head. "TV room, dudettes?"

"So we can see the Dude doom and gloom? Sure, why not? It may be the last time I ever get to see a TV again. I'll probably have to wear one of those satellite bracelets for the rest of my life. In solitary confinement."

"Briddish, I thought you had more guts than that. Look on the bright side," Christina says as we walk down the corridor and push open the TV room door.

"What bright side?"

"Okay, I admit it. I'm still trying to think of one. Do your stuff with the shielding, Zak."

"Yes, O mighty dudette," Zak says, and after he's done it, we switch on *The Apartment.*

"I threw out the lasagna," Dude's telling Peter as he loads the washing machine. "It's not helfy, eating food that's been hangin' around."

"It was only from last night, man, how could you throw away my breakfast? You're, like, obsessed."

"Word. Obsessed." Zoe comes stalking into the kitchen. "Where are my sheets? Because I'm guessing you have something to do with their missing status."

"They're in the washing machine, Zoe. You know I like the linens to be washed regularly."

"Why are you worried about my linens since you aren't actually sharing the bed with me? No, don't answer that. I give up. Just stay away from me, you crazy freak."

As the rest of *The Apartment*'s inhabitants appear and get into a huge row, my head begins to pound.

"Turn it off, I can't bear it," I say, feeling fear and panic squeeze my stomach.

"I know what you mean," Christina says. "You know, this is partly my fault."

"No, it's not, I was the one doing the compelling."

"But I dared you to do it. I'm an accomplice to the crime."

"I didn't try hard enough to stop you," April breaks in, nearly in tears. "We may never see you again after today."

"Dudettes, don't you think you're being totally wimpy and dramatic about this? You, especially," he says to Christina. "You're supposed to be the hard one."

Christina digs him in the ribs.

"Okay, that's better. You're back. Now come on, guys, group hug," Zak says, opening his arms. "What?" he asks Christina when she scowls at him. "You can't blame a guy for trying to hug his near-girlfriend, even if it is in a group situation."

"Who says I'm your near-girlfriend and not your real girlfriend?"

Zak grins at her. "So you want to hug me by myself?"

"Let's not run before we can walk. We'll try the group thing first."

It's nice and reassuring to be hugged, but it does have an air of finality about it. I may never see them ever again.

At that moment the TV room door opens and in walks Cristobel Lantigue. "I came to see how your bonding was going," she tells us in her dry, dusty voice. "I see that you have it well in hand." Then she leaves.

We all fall around laughing, but after we've stopped, April turns to me.

"You have to tell Will the truth."

Just like Gina and Joe said. Three's the charm.

Before Will arrives home, I worry that he will be so tired. I don't want to burden him with my story, yet burden him I must. I'd like to leave it until he's had a good night's sleep, but if I do that he'll see Naomi and Grandfather Rick, the products of my handiwork, in action. Also, I need to get this off my chest. I'll explode if I don't.

I'm waiting for him by the front door when Jessica pulls the Prius up in the driveway.

Naomi is upstairs creating her designs. Aunt Claire is out at her first charity function of the week. Before she left she asked me to make sure Naomi and I ate dinner, with an emphasis on Naomi, which is good, I suppose. Grandmother Gloria and Grandfather Rick are out to dinner by themselves. It was supposed to be our self-improvement night, and I could do with a lot of that, but Grandfather Rick had other ideas.

Oh, this whole mess is my fault.

"Fiona?" Will and Jessica ask simultaneously as they open the door and see me standing there.

I burst into tears. "I've done something really awful," I blurt.

Will enfolds me in his arms and leads me to the living room. He sits with me on one of Grandmother Gloria's Marie Antoinette sofas, Jessica following close behind.

"I might get tearstains on the pillow," I say in between sobs.

"Tearstains, shmearstains." Will hugs me and pulls my head against his chest. It's very comforting. "It's only an old sofa, we can always get another one. We definitely can't get another *you*, can we, Jess? Now what's so awful that it's gotten you this upset?"

"Do you want me to leave so you can have some privacy?" Jessica asks in a worried tone.

"No, you can stay to hear my shame," I say, hiccuping. "Everyone will know about it next week, anyway."

"I can't imagine it's that shameful," Will says gently.

"Shameful just isn't you," Jessica adds, patting my hand.

I tell them the whole story from start to finish. I begin with the alternative precognitive visions I had for Grandmother Gloria and Naomi. I tell them all about my willful acts of compulsion on them, I don't make any excuses, I shouldn't have been trying to use ESP away from Esper Hall. I don't try to apportion any blame to anyone but myself.

All the while, Will sits quietly and listens, his arm around me. Jessica sits quietly and listens, too, on the floor by my feet, her hand resting on my knee in a reassuring way. To be honest, on occasion, like when I explain about how I came to accidentally use my compulsion on Dude Mann via the TV, which is what gave me confidence for using my compulsion in the first place, I feel Will's chest shudder like he's laughing. Even Jessica stifles a smile. Or am I imagining it?

"So there you have it," I sob when I come to the last part with Grandfather Rick. "Now Grandmother Gloria's life is ruined, and she feels like drinking vodka and tomato juice for breakfast."

Will's chest moves at that one, too. And Jessica laughs out loud. "I think she might have been joking on that one. I told you your grandmother wasn't that bad."

"And Naomi's getting thinner, and soon she'll be nothing more than skin and bones. I wish I'd told you what was going on sooner," I sigh.

"I wish you had, too, sweetie, but you know what? I understand why you didn't." Will sighs, too. "I knew we had problems. I should have dealt with these family issues before, but I just didn't seem to ever have the time. I let them slide."

"I know—you're superbusy being a superhero."

"Too busy being a superhero for everybody but the people I love. I must take partial blame for what you did, if blame is the right word to use. It just seemed easier to defer dealing with family issues. And I must learn to delegate more. Other people could have taken this mission in California, but I felt responsible."

"You can't save the entire world," I say, smiling against his chest.

"He's certainly trying," Jessica says. "But you're right, Will, you do need to delegate more."

"You really are a hero, Dad." I hear his quick intake of breath as I call him that. "If that's okay for me to call you that."

"That's perfect with me." He kisses the top of my head.

"You know, I'll take any punishment that Esper thinks I deserve, including solitary confinement forever or wearing one of the special armband things that stops ESP and can be tracked via satellite for life."

At that, Will and Jessica burst out laughing again.

This is funny how?

"Oh, Fiona," he says, pulling me into his arms. "You're priceless."

I am? "You mean you're not mad at me?"

"I certainly should be." He takes a deep breath. "I have a secret to tell you. *Everybody*, but *everybody*, breaks the rules."

"They do?" I think of Jessica teleporting from her special location to her house in Manhattan. I think of Will's love vibes.

"It's human nature," Jessica tells me. "What we try to do with boot camp is to ensure you all have the knowledge and expertise to know when and how to do it, and how much power to use. And it's usually better to stay away from compulsion, unless it's gentle guidance away from harm."

"I still stand by what I said to you at the very beginning. It's best to go through life causing as little harm as possible to people," Will tells me, giving me another squeeze. "And sweetie, we're here for you, we're family. Just ask us for help in the future, because those precognitive visions can be wrong."

Dad's right. I don't have to do all this stuff alone, I have him and Jessica to turn to. And then another thought occurs to me. "Can I just ask you something? Do you emit love vibes when you want those around you to be happy?"

Dad's face is inscrutably sphinxlike as he answers me.

"Can't a guy keep a few love-vibe secrets?" Then he winks at me and Jessica.

"Fiona Blount, do you agree to succumb to a mind-reading test so that we can establish exactly what happened, and your motives for doing what was done?" Madeline Markovy asks me on Monday morning when the board of directors for boot camp is called to emergency session.

"Furthermore, do you agree to the final judgment of this board?" Herbert Rafaelle asks.

I look around the room. All of my teachers are here except for Jessica, because she had to recuse herself on the grounds of not being impartial.

I nod. I have no choice.

"And you understand that if you knowingly lie to us, the repercussions will be even more severe." Madeline Markovy, again. She still reminds me of Morticia Addams, even though she's always been nice to me. At least, she always used to be nice to me before *I* made a mess of things.

I nod again. I still have no choice.

"Tell your story, child. I mean, Fiona," Miss Bird adds and gives me an encouraging smile. That reassures me a bit.

So I tell them exactly what I told Will and Jessica on Friday night, from start to finish. And then I worry because I missed a bit.

"Um, I did nearly use my compulsion on another occasion," I say. "Does that count? Do you need to know what it was? See, it was a bit embarrassing." I'm thinking of when I nearly compelled the Hot Italian Babe to stay away from my boyfriend.

"No, we're only interested in the parts that actually happened," Madeline Markovy tells me. "Now sit here so that I can read your mind. Relax." She puts her hands on my head.

As she rummages around in my brain again, I get that totally weird feeling like when she was helping me to force through the barrier, when I was having trouble using my ESP. She's sifting through my memories, but how does she know the right ones to look at? What if she peeks at private stuff, like Joe kissing me?

"Relax," she tells me again. "I know what I'm doing. I won't look at anything I'm not supposed to."

Oh, I've made such a mess of things. After what feels like a million years, but is only a few minutes, she stops.

"I pronounce that Fiona's account is accurate." With that, Madeline Markovy returns to sit with the other teachers and they confer among themselves. Cristobel Lantigue glances over at me, and I shudder.

After all I've done, I deserve to be punished severely.

I mean, I know that Jessica, with the help of some empaths

and healers, has lifted the compulsion from Grandfather Rick and Naomi, but they don't seem back to their normal selves yet. Jessica says that it will take a few days to kick in, because she used gentle amounts of ESP. Unlike me when I was doing the actual compelling in the first place. They also compelled Dude via the TV.

The teachers all glance my way, and my heart is pounding through my rib cage. Mr. Rafaelle stands, and I hold my breath as they look at me.

"We pronounce you guilty," he announces, just as the room to the conference door is thrust open, and the two Esperteers and Z'Aktagnan stride in.

"What is the meaning of this?" Miss Bird jumps to her feet. "You shouldn't be in here; this is a closed hearing."

"Yeah, well, we know what it's about," Christina jumps in. "If there's any punishment being handed out, then I should get some, too," she declares. "I encouraged her to use her compulsion. Even though I knew it was wrong."

"You're my hero, dudette."

"Will you stop being all girly?" Christina elbows Zak in the ribs.

"I like him being girly," April says. "He's completely in touch with his feminine side." Then she turns to the teachers. "I knew about Fiona's compulsion, too, and I didn't say anything, so that makes me an accomplice."

"Silence." Cristobel Lantigue's voice booms around the room and we all jump. Who knew she had such a powerful pair of lungs? "Why is this relevant?"

"Well, du—" Zak begins, thinks about his choice of words, and pauses. "Well, Miss Lantigue, you know how you said that we should bond because one day our lives could depend on it?"

"We figured it meant today," April says.

Cristobel Lantigue's mouth twitches into a smile, then she suppresses it.

I am so touched by their concern, but the blame is all mine.

"But you didn't actually *do* anything," I say to them. Then, to the teaching board, "It was all me."

"But if there's any life imprisonment being handed down, then we want to share it," Christina says. "Well, not all of it, I'm not that soft, Briddish."

"This is highly unusual, *highly* unusual." Miss Bird and the teachers all huddle among themselves to talk again. After what feels like ages, Mr. Rafaelle stands up.

"Fiona Blount, you are hereby suspended for the last week of boot camp," Mr. Rafaelle announces, and we sigh collectively with relief. "You are also required to wear a dampening bracelet so that you can't use your ESP skills."

"That sucks," Christina says.

"Isn't that against the law or something?" April asks.

"You think any of this is legal?" Christina and I ask her at the same time, grinning at each other.

"To be honest, I think it's a good thing," I say. "I should never be allowed to use ESP ever again. I'm a public menace. Even though I'm really, really sorry."

"I do wish you wouldn't jump to conclusions," Mr. Rafaelle says, exasperated. "You'll only be required to wear the bracelet for one week."

I think that's very lenient.

"Um, thank you," I say.

"What about us?" April, Zak, and Christina ask almost simultaneously.

"The board commends you for your honesty," Cristobel tells them in her dry, dusty voice. And this time she lets herself smile.

Whew. Everything's back to normal!

When I say normal, I mean normal with a bit of a difference, but in a good kind of way. And, of course, I still feel completely guilty about what I did. Even after my week's suspension and wearing the bracelet. That was such a weird feeling, not being able to even gather my will to put up my shield. But this morning Jessica took it off before breakfast. Boot camp is officially finished.

"Your punishment is over," she told me, with a mock-stern expression. "Make good use of your freedom."

"I don't intend to do anything I'm not supposed to do ever again."

"Until the next time."

"No, never."

Anyway, I have two more weeks left here in America, and I'm going to spend them atoning for my sins.

I spent the morning with Grandfather Rick in the basement, as he finished inventing his toasted sandwich maker. I didn't have the heart to tell him it's already been invented. I've been spending every morning in the basement, as per my previous offer to listen and learn about every one of his inventions.

"I think this is ready," he booms at me. "What do you think, Fiona? Will you go and fetch everybody so that they can come and witness this revolutionary machine? Especially your grandmother, she'll hate it if she misses it."

Grandfather Rick still spends time upstairs, mainly for meals and some trips with Grandmother Gloria, but I think that's sweet. It's a nice balance now, and I wonder if Jessica only kind of fixed my original compulsion, leaving a bit in place.

"I think you've timed it well. Grandmother Gloria will have finished her important phone calls by now," I tell him and run upstairs to collect everyone. Except Will and Jessica. They're at work in Manhattan today. So it's just me, Grandmother Gloria, Aunt Claire, and Naomi. Unfortunately, the cutting-into-perfect-triangles part of the machine still doesn't work that well—the sandwich comes out in eight little mangled pieces.

Grandmother Gloria is really nice to him about it. "Eight is a very good number—each piece is small enough to be bite-sized," she tells him, taking a mouthful. "And it tastes good, which is the important thing."

"Excellent cheese, Grandfather Rick." I am thrilled that Naomi eats some, too. I can't believe she does, on account of cheese having all those calories in it, but when Aunt Claire and I look at her, she's all, "What? A little cheese is good for calcium. A woman of any age has to worry about calcium for her bones." Naomi's really eating normally again, even though I am watching every mouthful she has, just to be sure. Just this morning she ate breakfast like she'd never been on the path to anorexia and size zero.

"That's so true." Aunt Claire shakes her head, then goes on to tell us about people with nutrient deficiencies all around the world, as per usual.

Go, Naomi!

Grandmother Gloria just smiles (which makes her whole face look really normal and grandmother-ish, but still in a stylish, sophisticated kind of way) and says, "Naomi, you look beautiful today. Did you design and make that top yourself, darling?"

You could bowl me over with a feather! It just shows the effect a bit of attention and affection can have on a person.

Dude Mann isn't exactly a success story from the human morality point of view, but during the course of the week he did revert to his old self again, being a slob and generally talking to the disenfranchised, material youth of America. He didn't get voted off the show, much to my secret relief.

The other two Esperteers and Z'Aktagnan were relieved, too. We've been keeping in touch through e-mail and instant messages. All for one and one for all.

So, the only thing missing from my life right now is Joe. Not that he's missing, because we've spent so much time on the phone watching the static. Will bought me a TV and had a landline installed in my bedroom, just so I didn't have to watch static in the living room all the time.

On the one hand, I can't believe how quickly the month has gone, but on the other hand it feels like forever since I saw Mum and Mark Collingridge and Daphne Kat, and Gina and Peaceflower.

Actually, Joe and Gina have both been offline today, which is strange, because they usually check in to say at least hello on a daily basis.

They both sent me really odd e-mails last night, too.

To: "Fiona Blount" <MarieCurieGirl@bluesky.com>
From: "Gina Duffy" <Feminista@bluesky.com>
Subject: I wish

I wish I could see you. ;) ;)

She knows how I feel about wishing for anything these days, but it's nice that she's missing me. But Joe's was really cryptic.

To: "Fiona Blount" <MarieCurieGirl@bluesky.com>
From: "Joe Summers" <OccamsRazor@sciencenet.com>
Subject: Guess What I'm Doing This Summer?

You'll never guess in 13.7 billion years.

What's that supposed to mean? Not that he's back off to Italy, I hope, but I know better than that. Maybe it means that the summer feels 13.7 billion years long?

I finger Trilby as I walk upstairs in search of Naomi. She ran up to change for our swim.

As I climb the stairs, the front door opens, and I pause.

"Fiona, you upstairs?" Dad calls.

"I'm here," I say, dashing down the steps so that I can hug him.

And stop in my tracks.

Dad is not alone.

With him are Gina, Peaceflower, and Brian. And behind them is Joe!

"Surprise!" they all yell, and I'm engulfed in a group hug.

"I thought you'd like for your friends to spend some time with you," Dad says, grinning at me. "So I flew them out to see you."

"It was really hard not to give you a hint on e-mail or instant message," Gina tells me, throwing her arms around me. "You know what I'm like with secrets."

"I think you're fabulous with secrets," I tell her, because she is. After all, she hasn't told a soul about my ESP.

"Hi, Marie Curie Girl," Joe says, flashing me his enigmatic smile. He's all tall, even taller than he was a month ago if that's possible. And tanned. And his hair has gone all golden from the Italian sunshine. He's just beautiful, and in that moment I love him more than ever.

"You look gorgeous," he whispers to me, his voice full of emotion. "How's that for mushy?"

"Pretty good," I say as I throw my arms around him right there in front of everyone. Actually, it's totally fabulous.